AF487154

Rich

&

Bitter

N. Cole Burke

Table of Contents

At the time of writing this, I am neither.
I imagine that in fifty years I'll probably be one;

Preferably the first, rather than the latter.

OCTOBER

Rich Indeed

I haven't got a dollar,
I haven't got a dime,
But if you've got a minute,
I'll pay you with some time.

For deep inside my pockets,
Beneath the fairy dust grown old,
I've got here a shiny thimble,
Full of memories not yet told.

For you, a plump and lovely lass,
And your fellow, meek and lean,
I'll gladly share my treasures,
Of mysterious unknown things.

I've got a wallet full of owl whispers,
And a coin purse full of sleeping sand,
And my bank vault's full of stories,
The best in all the land.

No, I haven't got a dollar,
And I haven't got a dime,
I've made investments elsewhere,
And now I'm rich with time.

<u>Friends of Mine</u>

Death holds me like a lover,
Cruelty treats me like a friend,
And all I've ever known,
Are the places that we've been.

Murder, Wrath, and Mayhem,
Invite us out for tea.
And while my friends are gruesome,
They've all been kind to me.

Sadness likes to whittle,
And Darkness sails the bay.
Revenge is fond of games,
The worst of worst to play.

I've drowned cities with my tears,
And deafened countries with my screams.
You can keep your plastic heroes,
While I keep company with my fiends.

<u>***Dreamer Child***</u>

What is a dream,
But a mind spilling over.
Sloshed from a bucket,
And pooling on the floor.

What is a thought,
But madness woven.
Knots tied to dreams,
And sails flying away.

What is a mind,
But darkness and goblins,
And a stumbling strength,
Of dreams half-forgotten.

Still Waiting

Sitting on the curbside,
Wondering where he's been,
He said it'd be just a minute,
Buts gone well past ten.

He fought again with Mommy,
I hate it when they shout,
So out I go to sit,
And try not to think about.

The bruises on her cheek,
The perfume on his shirt,
The way the neighbors stare,
Like we're dirtier than dirt.

He's left so many many times,
But always he came back,
So, I sit there on the curb,
And watch the ants down in the crack.

The time it ticked so slowly by,
He said he was just gonna grab a beer,
He said he'd be just a minute,
Yet I've been waiting for sixteen years.

The Man in the Arena

In the vast colosseum's ring, he stands,
Moments before the fateful command,
No critic's voice can shake his core,
For he is the man the arena calls for.

With dust and sweat upon his face,
In this sacred space, he does embrace,
The weight of deeds yet to be done,
A warrior's hart thrills with battles to be won.

He strives valiantly, unyielding in his quest,
Though shadows of doubt may try to infest,
But in this arena, where heroes are made,
He'll face challenges, undeterred, unswayed.

The critics may whisper, their words may sting,
But he heeds not their hollow murmurings,
For it is the credit of valor that he seeks,
In this moment, his spirit dances and leaps.

[continued]

[The Man in the Arena-continued]

With each heartbeat, courage ignites,
Fueling his spirit, ready to fight,
In this arena, simple purpose he finds,
A noble cause that sharpens his mind.

Though stumbles may come, errors befall,
He rises again, to answer the call,
For he knows the triumph of the great,
Awaits the man who battles, undeterred by fate.

He spends himself freely, in this worthy case,
Body and soul, unyielding applause,
For the glory lies not with critics meek,
But in the struggle, where warriors speak.

In the face of defeat, if it should appear,
He'll fail daring greatly, with nothing to fear,
Never to join the cold souls of the tame,
But to rise again, undying in his aim.

So let the battle commence, the clash begins,
In this arena, where stories they spin,
He stands there now, with spirit aflame.
The man, the gladiator, a beast untamed.

Fear

It boils and slithers.
It creeps and crawls.
It chokes your heart,
And plagues us all.

Demented playmate.
Goddess of torment.
Damnedable fiend.
It makes a man repent.

Thief of peace,
Robber of breath,
Consumes your mind,
Until there's nothing left.

What foul master.
What a loathsome lot.
Infects you like a poison,
A waking, living rot.

<u>***Truth Remains***</u>

Dancing embers that suffocate,
To which the silent moon does call,
It's just a bit of broken glass,
That flew into the wall.

There's not a hollow memory,
That doesn't shriek so sound,
As that of the laughing moon,
When pillars come crashing down.

The fae folk like to whisper,
When taunting voices pass them by,
Those silly little human folks,
With embers in their eyes.

<u>*Whimsy*</u>

Could you not be a flea,
Today of all the weeks.
It's such a passing fancy,
Just like the bee's knees.

Or given a gay old time,
Was there not more to say?
It comes along then goes,
Like the growing of a nose.

Or a whistle in the wind,
Or a song sung in the heart.
Life's so full of mischief,
Like laughter in the dark.

What Then?

When the world runs out of pennies and
dimes,
What will all the rich men do?
They'll sit on their ass, and declare there's
a tax!
And steal all that they can from you.

When the world runs out of copper and gold,
What, oh what, will the rich men hold?
They'll hoard gobs of mud, still spilling blood,
And they'll bargain for what price you'll be
sold.

When the world runs out of power and greed,
What wisdom, then, will the rich men heed?
They'll listen not to word or thought,
For cursed are the rich men who can never be
freed.

The Weight of War

Harold, what have you done?
Handing that boy a gun.
Spoke of war like a game of fun,
Not of demons you can't outrun.
Harold, what have you done?

Harold, what have you done?
That boy was like a son.
And the battle may be won,
But you shall forever be shunned.
Oh, Harold what have you done?

Harold, what have you done?
Every soldier was once someone.
And death has bitterly stung,
Yet you keep on handing out guns.
Harold, when will this war be done?

Wallflower Warrior Song

Who am I but a fly on the wall?
Who am I but a moth to the flame?
A spirit forgotten, a name forsaken.
A rose, a storm, a chance not taken.

What all could I be if they only knew?
What passions awakened untainted and true?
A possibility beyond measure.
A rough road to weather.

Could there be more to the day than the
dawn?
More to the sparrow than just his song?
Could the ocean hold her beautiful
mysteries deep?
A light in the dark, a voice to speak?

<u>***D is for Disgraced***</u>

Drinking delicious dreams of delirium,
Darkness draped across the dangling door,
Detestable debauchery, laughing dishonesty,
Disgusted and disturbed, who could ask for
more?

Drugged drunk with dim disgrace,
Do or do not demonstrate demonic deeds,
Demolish this den of demented debris,
Domestic danger agrees to disagree.

Didn't deny the divine decree,
Didn't deny the drowning dawn,
Didn't deny the doom and discomfort,
Devoid and dismal once dusty duty has gone.

The Howling Grave

I planted Daisy Tuesday, beneath the
summer sun,
In a garden of my making. What has my
mind become?
The whispering wind called out my name,
Not a tinkling of bells, but a howling of
the grave.

A moan, a wail, I do not jest,
Commanding that I must confess.
Yet my mortal soul can not be saved,
So I ignore the howling of the grave.

Such a fate to suffer all,
And yet the pain I can't recall.
There's just the bliss that soon does fade,
When comes the howling of the grave.

[continued]

[The Howling Grave-continued]

It warns out there waits a plot for me,
For Death does own all victory.
Soon will be my time to pay,
So warns the howling, howling grave.

"For what? I have done nothing wrong!
'Cept plant some flowers in the lawn…"
I sense the wind knows I've misbehaved,
For I see it now! The howling grave!

Upon the hill I watch it creep.
A rotted creature of bone and meat.
"It's just a vision soon to fade."
I mumble beneath the howling grave.

I latch the door and half dare hope,
To fend it off with knife and rope.
To my demise the door concaves,
Beneath the claws of the howling grave!

I'd rather greet Death than the horror there,
With hungry eyes that into my soul do stare.
There comes a time when all debts are paid,
Best do it before comes the howling grave.

NOVEMBER

Artist of Us All

Dreaming dreams and listening,
To unspoken speeches inside my head.
Paintings, beautiful masterpieces,
Dancing above my bed.

I hear the call so beautiful,
It sends shivers down my spine.
Chaotic wisdom blossoming,
And yet I must toe the line.

For roses smell so sweet,
Given any other name.
And the prophets and the poets,
They don't give a damn for fame.

It matters not how little,
Or how muddled of a mess.
Graceful purpose of the arts,
Is to give your spirit rest.

A Thanks to All the Sacred Clowns

Painted man of humor,
Forced to smile all the time.
Hides tears and heartache alike,
With laughter for a dime.

Poet cursed with wisdom,
That no one will ever heed.
Juggles, jokes, and jests for us,
Despite his wounds that bleed.

We mock him every chance we get,
Without a thought, without a care.
Laughing as he flounders around,
Giggling as he gasps for air.

Oh painted man of humor,
Doomed with painful prophecy,
Tell me what harsh truth,
Will you share today with me?

[continued]

[A Thanks to All the Sacred Clowns-continued]

The sting of facts delivered,
With a playful teasing hand.
Will we feel the blows like rocks,
Or let them slip away like sand?

Teach us how to laugh at power.
Show us how to mock the crown.
Remind us of all that blinds us.
It is we who are the clowns.

<u>***WTF***</u>

There are times in my life when I've got
nothing to say,
And there are times in my life when people
just blow me away.
There are moments,
In our lives,
That make you wonder,
And right now I'm wondering "Why?"

What We Need

Wholesome Sam was a very clever man,
Who would know just what you need.
He sheltered the lost,
Provided warmth from the frost,
And any hungry belly he met he'd feed.

If a heart was hurt, he'd have a hug to spare.
He was patient, gentle, and kind.
Comforted folks when trouble came near,
The fat cats would scoff at his cheer,
But their words he never did mind.

Because Wholesome Sam wanted for nothing,
He could do just whatever he pleased.
He showed charity because he could.
He cared because he knew he should,
And he was rich because his heart was at ease.

These Friends I'll Keep

In a land where laughter meets the absurd,
I found myself in a place delightfully disturbed.
A journey led me down to the depths below,
Where disasters and chaos start to grow.

With a mischievous grin and a wicked
charm,
I wandered through Hell, causing such an
alarm,
Demons and devils, all gathered around,
A rowdy bunch, the loudest in town.

They danced and they laughed, oh what a sight,
In this fiery realm, where day turns to night,
The flames danced high, casting an ominous
glow,
And cackling chuckles blew like a chilling snow.

At least in Hell I'll find good company,
Where no one fears what they are or be.
The demons and criminals gave a riotous
 cheer.
With disastrous laughter that filled the air.

[continued]

[These Friends I'll Keep-continued]

We played pranks on the bitter folks who
loved despair,
Their moans and groans, a sound so
incredibly fair,
We painted the flames with colorful delight,
Turned pitchforks into confetti, oh what a
sight!

In this strange place, where chaos reigns
supreme,
I found joy and camaraderie, a beautiful
dream.
In the depths of Hell, where laughter's set
free,
At least in Hell, you'll find good company.

Things I've lost and things I've found,
Horribly unbalanced now.
A shiny penny can't undo,
All the time that I could have spent with you.
Wasted away on work and stress,
Forgetting mortality is what we're all blessed.
Now my hands hold faded wisdom,
Washed away like a crumbling prison.
For had I only known back then,
I'd pick a different lot of friends.
Instead, I anchored down with panic and fear,
Anxiety's whispers were all I could hear.
While out the window Joy went about so
merrily,
And Bliss and Hope looked on so carefree.
All the while I hid away,
Filled with worry of what others would say.
Or think! Dear lord, what might others think!
The thought alone could push me to the brink!
There are so many things that I've lost,
By far, Time had the worst cost.
For now, I sit here, all run down,
Rich and bittered by the things I've found.

<u>*At Ease*</u>

Forests of bones and rivers of blood,
Here comes the fire, here comes the flood,
Washes rivers down the mountain slopes,
Fortress strong, born of rock and rope,
Tangled webs with lies we weave,
Spinning dreams into reality,
The trumpet sounds, it's time to run.
Fires the cannon, thunders the gun,
Fast of foot, fast of flame,
Fast of death, slow to blame,
Pain races up, just like a train,
Chills sprinkle down, just like the rain,
Lay down the weapon, lay down the head,
Lay down to rest among the dead.

Fame or Fortune

Hope doesn't feed a hungry belly,
And wishes don't pay the bills,
Dreams are nice,
But best think twice,
Before selling it all for thrills.

These stones I know, they speak the truth,
And though they are far from kind,
They stood their ground,
Forever sound,
They are the foundation of my mind.

And tempting as the fairytale might be,
To be the popper transformed into a king,
Logic shall rule,
I'll never be fooled,
I shall be content in life with simpler things.

Carry On My Wayward Son

We all need a little crash and burn,
To rise from the ashes and fly like a bird,
They say it's not the fall that kills you,
it's the staying down,
We are all lost until we are found.

You gotta fail to succeed and fall to rise,
There is no redemption without the lies,
What makes being perfect so damn good?
When it's the broken man who's best
understood.

To have been to the bottom and climbed to
the top,
To have taken chances and suffered lose,
We're all sinners in our own ways,
That is the beauty, that is our grace.

Crash and burn and fall again and again,
Stumble but carry on, until the very end.

<u>The Face of Eternity</u>

The moor at midnight plagues my soul,
Bitter laughter, of dark and icy cold,
Sweetest whisper from starlight sky,
And for a moment, with wings I fly,
Into the never-ending nothing of the night,
Into the face of phantom figured frights,
We dance and laugh and sing and love,
Then like rain we tumble from up above,
Crash through the clouds like forgotten grace,
Smash and smack and ripped like lace,
Tattered spills and sorrowful woes,
A voyager guided by where the wind blows,
Explorer of mountains and namer of trees,
Friend of the madman never dared set free,
Darkness, lover, minister of men,
Echoing open emptiness without end.

<u>*All of Me*</u>

They pick the rose for her beauty,
And curse her for her thorns.
"You can have the best of me," says she,
"But you must take the rest of me," says she.

They marvel at the sunrise,
But tremble at the night,
They delight in the victory,
But ridicule the fight.

They love the rainbow and all his colors,
But complain about the storms and rains.
"You can have the best of me," says he,
"But you must take the rest of me," says he.

They love the feather but not the bird,
They hate the clam but love the pearl,
They love and hate and hate and love,
As if there were two separate things.

For there can be no perfection, without a
bitter sting.

Action Speaks Louder

It matters not the truth you tell,
It matters not how loud you yell,
When lies taste so much sweeter,
When you fight against a cheater.
You can shower them with proof,
Doesn't matter, what's the use?
All the science, all the facts,
When power's what you truly lack,
They'll paint you just another fool,
If you decided not to be their tool,
Or dare to question or dare to think!
Cause a commotion, cause a stink.
They hate it more than they can bare,
A soul so unique, a mind so rare,
It matters not what you say,
They'll brush it all away,
So perhaps it's time to try once more,
To level the field and even the score,
It seems high time we show them,
Maybe then they'll start to listen,
They'll see then, we're here to stay,
And best they change their wicked ways.

It Comes

The wind is howling so angrily, I think it
forgot to be fed,
Tauntingly teases mercilessly, there are
monsters beneath my bed,
The chill sobers heart and soul, the gray takes
my breath away,
It's a bleeding twilight wonder, half night time
and half day.

The mind slips a step backwards, lost as it
reminisces,
The breeze caress softly, like gentle biting
kisses,
The ground sags beneath my boots, leaves
spin all around,
The stillness of all the world, gives a deafening
sound.

[continued]

[It Comes-continued]

What has come now must go as into tomorrow
I step,
It is a time of reflection, and the wind is the
one who wept,
Icy tears splash my face, cautioning of coming
storms,
This is the season of eternal slumber, and we've
all just been warned.

The trick to surviving Hell is to walk through forests and flames alike.

DECEMBER

<u>*White Christmas*</u>

Couldn't be tomorrow, or better yesterday,
Couldn't come in gently, no it had to come today,
Two feet tall, no three, no six.
Standing at the window shrieking, "Now what the hell is this?!"
In the time it took to bundle up,
It's now spilling over from the cup.
"Who pissed off Santa?" I want to scream,
But the snow and wind are deafening.
This isn't what Hallmark promised me!
As we scrap and dig ourselves out free.
Where are the snowmen and hills for sleds?
Where's the roaring fire and plums dancing over beds?
This isn't what we all imagined when we prayed for snow to come,
Trapped inside this frozen hell. Thank God we still have rum!

<u>*As I Pass By*</u>

Cold hands and blue lips,
And skin a waxy gray.
I was born once in November,
Yet they lay me down in May.

It's not the fairness of the lot,
This hand that I've been dealt.
Winter robbed me something wicked,
Yet I'll return when summer's felt.

Had Death been any kinder,
He'd waited for next spring.
But such is not to be my fate,
Ain't life such a funny thing?

<u>*Esteem*</u>

Do you love me?
She asked the boy,
Who just pushed her in the mud.

Do you love me?
She asked her schoolmates,
Who teased her all day long.

Do you love me?
She asked her parents,
Who acted as if they hadn't heard.

Do you love me?
She asked the man,
Who left blue bruises out of sight.

Do you love me?
She asked her friend,
Who always always canceled plans.

[continued]

[Esteem-continued]

Do you love me?
She asked the baby,
Who could only sleep and cry.

Do you love me?
She asked the mirror,
Who could not bear reply.

<u>*Vile*</u>

I let out a scream,
That split apart the world,
And out poured monsters
You've hardly ever heard,

Of evil and perversion,
That could scarcely hold a name,
Oh how their crushing power
Quickly won them fame,

They gobbled up the children,
And washed them down with greed,
Cursed prophets with great wisdom,
That nobody would ever heed,

Ripped apart young girls,
Then dragged them through the dirt,
Painted saints of sinners,
Blaming crimes upon a skirt,

[continued]

[Vile-continued]

Stole babies from their mother's arms,
And had the gall to throw the blame,
Lived safely tucked in ivory towers,
But preaching we're all the same,

They grew so fat,
They grew so large,
They squashed the people,
They choked the stars,

They ate and ate and ate and ate,
Until there was nothing left,
Then there came a scream,
That left a dagger in their breast.

<u>*Ache*</u>

The breath has left my lungs,
And spills out on the floor.
A ghost that likes to linger,
I can't hold on anymore.

It was a whisper when it started,
But oh, how swiftly it did grow.
A burning, bleeding, twisting,
A weight, a brick, a moan.

A tumor lodged at the back of my throat,
A choking iron-handed grip.
Squeezes the heart.
Bites and rips apart.

<u>*Betrayal*</u>

Stone cold. Haunted yellow.
A different time. A gruesome fellow.
A young child's naivete.
A cold and windy autumn day.

Trust so easily given, quickly lost.
And innocence paid the cost.
Bloody greedy hungry heart.
Oh, but that's only just the start.

Sank low the blow like pirate ships,
When tempting words lured from those lips.
Lies and spies and friends turned foe.
Oh little child, how could you know?

Little Red Riding Hood

Lurking shadows, darkness coiled,
He watches all those that dare pass by.
Waiting, tempted, patiently,
What prey today will catch his eye?
They scream in horror at the sight of him.
He laughs, as scream they should.
Pulls them off the beaten path,
Thus becoming the wolf in the woods.

Red of flowers, berries, and of love,
Mother warns about red of blood.
She smiles and slips on her hood.
Warnings never did her any good.
Grabs her basket and off she goes.
A familiar walk where oak trees grow,
And perhaps along the way,
There'll be a woodsman with eyes of gray.

[continued]

[Little Red Riding Hood-continued]

He smiles and watches as she walks,
She doesn't recall, but once they talked.
They never notice him, no not at first,
But they never forget him once he's done his
worst.
She's pretty, then again aren't they all?
At least at first, before they fall.
His smile grows to manic glee,
She stops to rest behind a tree.

Mother would be so displeased with her.
She'd never be allowed out again, that's for
sure.
If luck is with her, and her timing is just right,
Their paths might cross in the midmorning
light.
Grandmother's house is really oh so very near,
She plans to venture off- Oh! But what's this
she hears?
Strange moans from the house, nay they are
shouts.
She must go and see what it's all about.

[continued]

[Little Red Riding Hood-continued]

Grandmother's not in her bed,
And all she sees is red red red.
Then shadow falls upon her and all is dark.
Away a gray-eyed woodsman hears a bark.
All is lost, yes this will be the end.
He'll have revenge on all that dare offend,
His manic hands that thirst for gore,
Then something slams against the door.

They never found the wolf in the woods,
However, it seems that he's gone for good.
She still wears red and walks dirt trails,
Her basket tied with a long black tail…

The Politician

Gray fox likes to whisper,
Telling fairy tales and lies.
Weaving webs of falsehoods,
Playing spider and the fly.
It takes no strain of thought,
To see the glimmer in his eyes.
Sheep assume with all his barking,
His ideas must be very wise.

Perhaps it matters little,
The tall tales we like to tell.
The truth is really nothing,
Just the stories that we sell,
To whoever pays the highest price.
It's the game we like to play,
And those that emerge victorious,
Decide what people say.

[continued]

[The Politician-continued]

It never sat that well with me,
The gray fox and his lies.
While crow with all his wisdom,
Is always pushed off to the side.
Cawing out dear warnings,
Desperate to fix the wrongs.
Gray fox likes to laugh and mock,
Says crow is just singing songs.

<u>*Bedfellows*</u>

Loneliness is cold,
Like waters that run deep.
It trickles, trickles slowly,
Like a wound that wants to bleed.

Misery is silent,
Just as quiet as they come.
It fidgets there so patiently,
Then up it bolts to run.

Regret it burns.
Hot, it claws and bites.
There's no escaping the torment,
That comes calling in the night.

<u>***The Simpleton***</u>

A chuckleheaded ninny,
Well, there are worse things I could be,
Like cruel or mean or scoundrel,
But feel free to disagree.

Yes, my head is up in the clouds,
And I rather like it there.
Perhaps you'd like to join me?
But would you ever dare?

My heart is on my sleeve,
And I say just what I think.
Why does that bother you?
Why go and make a stink?

Yes, there's darkness in the world,
And hoodlums all around,
But I'd rather see the good.
Listen to the heart's peaceful sound.

<u>*For the People*</u>

He walks along,
With one shoe gone,
And not a care in the world.

Save for the growl in his belly,
He's cold and he's smelly,
He's the vagrant at the end of the road.

Little children take caution,
When you fail in this nation,
People treat you worse than a dog that might
bite.

It's what we all fear,
But what few people hear,
The status of human comes with a price.

<u>***Presage***</u>

It tingles down the back,
Like lightning in the spine.
It whispers worried warnings,
Someone's crossed the line.

That feeling in the air,
Something wicked this way comes.
Omen, foreshadowing,
Of danger you can't outrun.

What Keeps You?

What keeps you up at night?
Is it secrets you didn't tell?
Or lies you told,
To fools for gold.
Oh, honey, I know them well.

Maybe it's the days now gone.
Those blissful memories,
Now empty melodies,
For sorrow is the sweetest song.

Perhaps it's tomorrow and all the worry it will
bring.
Decisions you must make.
Risks you're forced to take.
What keeps you up at night are all the little
things.

Every person has a price. Know yours.

JANUARY

__Redemption__

Birth and death and life and love,
Transformation rains from above.
The young and old reset renewed.
The past pushed out for tomorrow's to-dos.

The ball falls down, the crowd roars and
cheers.
It's not just a new day, it's a new year.
A new time, a new place, a new you.
Change your life, change your world, change
your view.

The magic to start again,
Is ever present, all around.
But on this blessed day,
It fills the air with a cheerful sound.

And some may stumble, trip and fall,
And some may strive and have it all.
Don't surrender each time you fail,
Rush to catch the ship before it sails.

<u>Careless</u>

There are words that were spoken in passing,
That to this day still haunts me to my core.
Gestures, jokes, and seemingly trifle matters,
That robbed my peace and caused reality to
blur.

It might not have meant a thing to them.
In fact, on that matter, I'm very certain.
To them, it was there in an instant gone in a
flash,
But for me, their weight was a heavy burden.

The mutter under someone's breath to leave,
The heavy sigh or roll of their eyes.
Admittedly it's my attention that gave them
power,
Yet the blows still hurt like bitter goodbyes.

Goodbye to the person I thought you were.
Goodbye to the version of me and you.
Goodbye to the peace I once held.
Welcome treasured solitude.

<u>*Death of a Child*</u>

Is this what getting older is?
The blush falling from the bloom.
The brightness of the world now muted.
There is only the dark and gloom.

A weariness that carries with it,
Apathy, cold and bare.
Forgotten are the days of youth,
Filled with excitement rare.

Eyes full of mystery and wonder,
Heart thirsting for adventures to explore.
Whatever happened to that happy child?
I don't see him in me anymore.

Sleepless

Crystal-clear uncertainty,
Comes crashing down on top of me,
And races round red ribbon doors.
Claws the walls and the floors,
Into the embers to suffocate,
And wonder what the world will see.
If there can only be tomorrow,
Then go ahead and let it be.

Child of January

Child of January, child of January,
The shameless revolutionary.
Patron saint of sanctuary,
Healer, savior, of all who be.

Child of February, scholar of fantasy,
Past and future you shall foresee.
Empathetic psychic cursed to be.
All that you hold is just temporary.

Child of March what shall you do?
There is no option in being number two.
Nothing else matters if the ribbon's not blue.
Victory is the only thing that speaks true.

Child of April, born of luxury rare,
Whose first priority is always self-care,
Then fussing over what to wear.
They haven't a moment at all to spare.

[continued]

[Child of January-continued]

Child of May, so curiosity-driven.
Both a roaring lion and a purring kitten.
Seeker and sounder of all things hidden.
Author of all that was left unwritten.

Child of June where did you go?
Ventured off where others dare not follow.
Preservation a lesson that they well know.
Alone in the garden is where they grow.

Child of July, royal and radiant as the sun.
In the spotlight, you can easily find them.
Burn bright as a day that's just begun.
The game of life they've already won.

Child of August who works so hard,
Labor and logic are all they regard,
And they're impossible to bombard.
Disciplined better than the finest guard.

[continued]

[Child of January-continued]

Child of September, the balancer of scales.
Harmony, peace, and justice will always
prevail.
Every yin has a yang, just like a hammer has a
nail.
It always evens out, down to the smallest of
details.

Child of October cloaked in elusive mystery,
Forever misunderstood they are cursed to be.
Born to be the villain and named the enemy.
Roam the haunted hills, laughing at eternity.

Child of November, the fearless adventurer.
Never travels back to where they've been
before.
Restless soul twisting, hungering for one more.
Always longing for an unfamiliar shore.

Child of December, keeper of the time.
Steady perseverance is the way they climb.
Every dollar that they made once was just a
dime.
Industry and zeal are their favorite prayers to
chime.

<u>*Open Wound*</u>

The hurt is fresh,
Though the blood may be old.
And there is no victory,
Without some pain, or so I'm told.

It's hard to think one step forward,
It's hard to see.
The sting has cut me deep,
It's hard to breathe.

Is this the end?
I half dare wish it to be.
Then again, perhaps,
It is just the beginning.

<u>***Un Ordinary***</u>

What better explains the trouble I'm always in,
Than the thirsting of a forever-hungry mind?
The twisted, crazy, morbid, messy ways,
Are my most favorite treasures to find.

I see the others so calmly marching.
Cookies cut for balanced scores.
Life would be so much easier,
If I didn't reach for something more.

Instead, I search for where the green grass grows,
I look for mystery, monsters, and mayhem alike.
While others enjoy the monotone monotony,
I delight with the sparks of forbidden fright.

A deck of cards weathered by the same old shuffle.
A narrow path worn down to the roots and rocks.
Instead I think I shall walk the streets backwards,
And see what new thoughts I can unlock.

The Foxhole at Dawn

Boom goes the cannons. Rata-tat goes the guns.
Careful now boys, here they come.
Slipping and spilling like snakes over the hill,
Before the day breaks, camouflaged with the chill.

Did you hear it? That hollow echoing howl.
Did you feel it? The evil enemy prowls.
Keep your eyes open, and your knife at the ready.
Careful now boys, keep those hands steady.

[continued]

[The Foxhole at Dawn-continued]

They slip through the trees like the whispers of
ghosts.
You can squirm with dread and fear but hold
your posts.
Was that one of them? That darting shadow
there.
Was that one of them? That dark mist in the
air.

Be ready boys, and pray your feet are quick.
Be ready boys. I know that you're homesick.
Just do this last deed and get the job done.
And maybe, just maybe, the war will be won.

<u>***Golden Flames***</u>

What pretty chains,
You wear them so well.
And your golden carriage,
Headed straight for hell.

Your bejeweled crown,
A thing of beauty.
For your shining treasures,
You abandoned your duty.

I hope you enjoyed it,
Your fortune and fame.
Remember them fondly,
As you sit in the flames.

<u>*Generations*</u>

One day man made a man,
And he said to him,
"You are man-made."

The made-man then made a man,
And he said to him,
"You are a man, made by the made-man."

This man, made by the made-man,
In turn, made himself a man,
And he said to him,
"You are a man, made by the made-man the
made-man made."

Then, as things go, the man,
Made by the made-man the made-man made,
He too made a man.

And the man, made by the made-man the
made-man made,
Looked at the man he made,
And he said to him,
"You are Doug."

When the Car Came for Me

In the midst of chaos, I stand alone,
Confusion gripping my heart, my home.
Voices of strangers echo all around,
As they tear me away, reason unfound.

Mommy's tears fall like rain, staining her face,
Fear paints her eyes, a desperate embrace.
I reach out, longing for her warm touch,
But they pull me away in a tight clutch.

The car door opens, my tiny heart pounds,
As I'm placed inside, lost in unfamiliar
sounds.
The engine roars to life, a deafening cry,
A world unraveling, as we say goodbye.

Questions swirl in my mind, like a storm so
mean,
Why must I leave? Is this a nightmare dream?
Will Mommy find me? Will she be okay?
As we drive away, I silently pray.

[continued]

[When the Car Came for Me-continued]

The road stretches before me, a path
unknown,
Leaving behind everything I've ever known.
I grip my small hands, eyes filled with despair,
Lost in this nightmare, overwhelmed by the
air.

Through the window's glass, I glimpse my
past,
A fading picture, a bond that, sadly, can not
last.
Mommy's silhouette fades in the distance,
I yearn for her touch, for her familiar
existence.

Inside this metal cage, my heart cries out,
Longing for comfort, surrounded by doubt.
The world rushes by, a blur of unknown,
As I embark on this journey, no place my own.

[continued]

[When the Car Came for Me-continued]

The ache in my chest, the knot in my throat,
As I navigate this path, so foreign and remote.
Who will protect me, hold me when I weep?
As I'm taken away, into the mysterious deep.

My heart is heavy, burdened by the weight,
Of separation's anguish, a sorrowful state.
And though fear may linger, casting its shade,
I still carry the love, the memories we made.

Why is this happening? Why are strangers
here?
Why are they blind to all of my fears?
They say I'm rescued, but I feel so damned.
Please help this child to understand.

Tick Tock

We never had a chance,
I always thought you knew.
The world it spins a backwards,
The old racing to be born anew.

So it is destiny as they say,
For us to wind the clock.
Yet these jokers laugh at us,
Farmers and we're their stock.

To kill ourselves so they might live,
On top of hills in houses of gold.
They robbed us of our youth,
Forgetting we all grow old.

The Failure's Hope

I screwed up, I'll admit it, and then there's
that,
That mess I made like a bothersome cat.
It's not so simple as saying you're wrong,
Especially when it becomes the same old song.
I can't really say which is the worse,
The knowing you tried, or knowing you're
cursed.
At the very least, these mistakes I'll confess,
But it hurts that I can't fix this bothersome
mess.
I'm sorry, I'm wrong, I apologize,
For the pain and the dirt and all the lies.
A screw-up, a jinx, I go by these names,
My faults and my failures my shining fame.
Glass vases turn to shards in my hands,
Stone bricks crumble just link the sands.
Time slugs on, each minute an agony,
Such is my fate, ever so sadly.
Yet I rise up each morning, more mistakes to
be made,
For yesterday's over, ad today's a new day

The most bitterly beautiful thing about life is
that nothing here is permanent.

FEBRUARY

<u>***Speak***</u>

I'm dying on the inside,
But then again, aren't we all?
Says the boy,
Says the girl,
Says the madman at the wall.

And we never really know,
The voices inside someone else's head.
And it's both tragedy and delight,
And a wonder about what's said.

That we waste so many words on frills,
Plastic passing phrases.
"Good day," "How are you?",
They're all a muck
Instead I crave richer flavors.

[continued]

[Speak-continued]

Speak to me of the monster,
That answers by your name.
Talk of the dancing shadows,
And the daring games you play.

Tell me all your greatest fears.
Tell me why you think you're weak.
Tell me of your saddest burdens.
Dear God, how I long to hear you speak!

Enraptured

Your lips look like a tasty treat,
A snack, my darling, I soon shall eat.
Your hair is a river my hand wishes to wade.
Enchanting forest in which my fingers can
play.
Your eyes are fires that warm my heart.
They pierce me sharper than any dart.
Your scent envelopes and intoxicates,
Leaves me weak, makes me quake.
You are a demon goddess, both to worship
and to fear,
And you are so much more than the flesh that
you appear.
Your laughter is a husky music, of drunken
twilight embers.
Your tongue cuts so cleverly, makes any man
surrender.
Your mind and wit are second-match to
absolutely none.
Your spirit is made of equal parts, scolding
nun and harlot's fun.
Enchant me, Temptress, let your beauty
breathe life into me.
If you ever settle for a fool, then gladly will
your fool I be.

Burn

Ready, yet?
Dear God, yes.
The match is set.
Burn the bridges down.

With trembling hands,
Hearts crumble like sand,
Wilt like forgotten land,
Like a storm without a sound.

We take the leap,
So our secrets we can keep.
Never again to sleep,
We sink deep under the ground.

No turning back,
In this fiery track,
Always under attack.
Where can peace be found?

Into a world we don't know.
Into the dark and the cold we go.
Just like a fire longs to grow,
We'll burn the bridges down.

Love's Bitter Death

Love lingers on the lips,
While hatred hollows out the heart,
And though they don't yet know it,
A war's about to start.

Fire burns the skin,
Like fingers along my flesh,
And once where there was love,
Now the dead lay down to rest.

It wasn't all our doing,
Though our indifference played a part.
Love withers like a flower,
When hatred hollows out the heart.

Love and Lies

In a moment of tenderness, she whispered,
Words that danced upon her tongue softly
delivered.
"She told him that she loved him," the story
goes,
Like a fragile rose, it was the sweetest lie she
ever told.

In her eyes, he saw the glimmer of affection,
A mirage of love, an irresistible connection.
Yet deep within her heart, a secret she
concealed,
A truth that in time would be revealed.

For in the depths of her soul, doubts resided,
Her love, a fabrication, a charade well-guided.
She spoke the words he longed to hear,
But her heart remained distant, filled with
fear.

[continued]

[Love and Lies-continued]

She spun a web of beauty, a fragile illusion,
Hoping to shield him from the depths of
confusion.
But every whispered "I love you" bore a
hidden sting,
The weight of deceit, like a delicate
heartstring.

And so their love story unfolded, a fragile
game,
With a lie at its core, a flickering flame.
"She told him she loved him," the tale echoes,
Her heart in throws over the sweetest lie she
ever told.

For in her silent torment, she couldn't let go,
Bound by the deception she chose to bestow.
In the depths of her soul, guilt began to reside,
As she lived a love built on a beautiful lie.

Empty Sorry

What good is a 'sorry' when the hurt is still there?
Like you don't even feel it. Like you don't even care.
To this blistering pain of mine, you're so unaware.
Gone is the ground. Gone is the air.
I gave you my heart. My life to share,
But this wound you gave, I can not bear.
I thought our love was a treasure so rare,
I thought we were such a befitting pair.
Yet you dashed those dreams with your love affair,
And though I long to forgive you, I do not dare.
For loving you will bring me only despair,
So with a heavy heart I simply must declare:
While your charm and beauty are Heavenly fair,
Your eyes of enchantment, your silken hair,
Like a summoned angel to answer prayers,

[continued]

[Empty Sorry-continued]

I shall spread the word for all to beware.
Your intoxication leaves one completely
impaired,
Never knowing if it's forever or just a flare.
I'd rather be married to sweet solitaire,
Then spend all of my nights wondering where,
Where you are, who you're with. It's such a
scare,
And so before again my heart you ensnare,
I make this oath, a vow I swear;
You may search for my heart, but it's no
longer there.

When a Heart Gets Broke

It ain't pretty when a heart gets broke,
Shattered pieces scattered like a cruel joke,
The pain seeps deep, like a relentless ache,
Leaving scars upon the soul, a bittersweet
wake.

Fragile dreams once held in tender embrace,
Now lost in the shadows, without a trace,
Love's delicate threads unraveled, torn apart,
Leaving behind a wounded and frail heart.

The echoes of laughter, now silenced and still,
The void within, an emptiness that can't be
filled,
Tears flow freely, a river of despair,
As heartache paints a picture so unfair.

[continued]

[When a Heart Gets Broke-continued]

But in the brokenness, a strength emerges,
A resilience that with time once again surges,
For through the pain, a spirit starts to mend,
Learning to rise, to heal, to transcend.

From the fragments, a new beauty is born,
A heart transformed, weathered but not torn,
In the mending, a wisdom softly spoken,
That even in heartbreak, a spirit can't be
broken.

So, let the tears fall, let the healing flow,
For it's in the healing that strength will grow,
It ain't pretty when a heart gets broke,
When it goes up in flames, a phoenix of
smoke.

<u>*Trauma*</u>

There's no crueler act than kindness,
When abuse is all you've ever known.
There's no misery so bitter,
When its compassion you are shown.

Or perhaps I should speak of laughter,
That pierces like bullets in the rain.
You're never sure if they're just mocking,
And there is no greater pain.

Of friendship, you find foreign,
And of peace, you've known just war.
These devils you've grown up with,
Just pimps and you're their whore.

Equality left you feeling lost,
Abandoned by the world.
For where were they when all around you,
Angry words and hurting hands did swirl?

For you, compassion is a weakness,
Beaten out of you from birth.
To be a cold unyielding stone,
That thinks violence gives you worth.

Could Have Been Love

We could have been a dream,
Brighter than the grandest jewel.
Instead, we were just common,
Nothing more than love blind fools.

Had we only known back then,
We could have been a dream.
Instead, we were like falling stars,
Thinking it was more than it seemed.

But the truth had us blushing,
Realizing there's more to love than crushing.
Had we only seen,
We could have been a dream.

<u>***First Heartbreak***</u>

"Are you stupid," said the man,
To the child who struggled to understand.
He didn't see the way their lips quivered.
Didn't care that they whimpered and shivered.

"Are you stupid," asked the man,
To the child who could not comprehend.
He didn't see the darkness in them grow.
He didn't know that inside sadness flowed.

"Are you stupid," called the man,
To the child who failed to follow commands.
He didn't realize that down deep inside,
That child's heart had slowly died.

"Are you stupid," sneered the man,
To the child when away they ran.
He didn't think of a heart that breaks,
And how sometimes to live, one must escape.

Beautiful Boy

Look at the hero just sitting there.
Not a care in the world,
Besides the curl in his hair.
Scold him, do you dare?

His chest is wide open.
Heartbroken explosion.
Morbidly is he.
Mind over matter?
She was the Cain to his Abel,
That animal.

Past the point of a phase.
Worse, it hurts.
This curse, those jerks.
Smiling with tears in his eyes,
He cries.
Can't hide the pain that he feels.
He thought her feelings were real.

[continued]

[Beautiful Boy-continued]

But can't hide behind lies like,
She said she was sorry a million times.
But still he tries,
To love her.
Til death do them part.
Duct Tape can't fix his broken heart.

Just a beautiful face.
Nothing underneath.
Cause she drilled it into his head,
And poured out all his 'stupid' dreams.
Now he's just her hero sitting there,
Only concern is for the curl in his hair.
Yet he'd rather be a zero with a dream,
Than the hero with the prom queen.

<u>*Live*</u>

Dare to take chances, dare to dream.
Dare to think of all the impossible things.
Dare to roar loud in the still of the silence.
Dare to be a rebel, proudly defiant.

And shoot for the moon and reach for the
stars.
And live your life free from all that bars,
That close you in and shut you down,
That ties you up, makes you feel like a clown.

It's a burning bleeding blessing.
Cold and hard and loved.
It is a twisted knotted jumbled mess.
Tainted masterpiece not yet carved.

<u>*Jealousy*</u>

Beware the green-eyed monster,
Who whispers in your ear all day.
He loves to get you going.
Torture is how he likes to play.

Beware the green-eyed monster,
And the twisted lies he sells.
His words may sound so smart,
But they pave the road to hell.

Beware the green-eyed monster,
For there is no greater harm,
Than one who sees only darkness,
And poisons peace with false alarm.

Love is not a feeling but a choice. And the
hardest one you'll ever make.

MARCH

<u>Beauty & the Beast</u>

A face bewitching to all.
Drew you in, made you fall.
Skin so soft and eyes that danced.
A smile that made you take a chance.
His was a beauty that knew no bounds,
Yet true love was never found,
For when you're cursed with a pretty face,
Genuine feelings flee from that place.

A face offending to all.
Stare in horror, hide behind walls.
Piglet's nose and protruding tusks.
What is the opposite of lust?
People are so quick to be snide, so quick to be
cruel.
When you look like a dog, you're treated
worse than a fool.
Hearts turn bitter, hearts turn cold.
It matters not your palaces of gold.

[continued]

[Beauty & the Beast-continued]

A stormy night, by chance or fate,
For two so different to meet at a gate,
And each looks upon the other,
And each takes pause and for a moment
wonders;
For who could ever love a beast,
When on beauty is all they wish to feast?
And beauty's wish for something more akin,
To crawling out of his own skin.

Dark forest hid the bitter light of day,
And two can speak all they wish to say.
To live life in a world so blind,
A loving heart is scarce to find,
But alone in the woods the two have found,
A kindred heart that loves unbound.
Day has come and the two depart,
But smile at their storming hearts.

[continued]

[Beauty & the Beast-continued]

Return again many days, many nights,
For a moment the world has been set to right.
Yet such happiness is doomed from the start,
For jealousy has poisoned a dangerous heart.
Into the woods beauty goes,
Unaware that he's been followed.
A creature with a mind as twisted as his heart,
Who draws a bow, with an arrow sharp.

Falls the beast among the leaves,
And away the madman goes and flees.
Beauty weeps but it matters not,
Beast was dealt a fatal shot.
Tears rain down on her mutant face,
But not a second would she replace.
As great a love, the tighter you grip,
Away great loves the world will rip.

<u>*Challenge Your Heart*</u>

People of darkness, monsters of light,
I wonder about the secrets you hide.
Smoke and shadows and slight of hand,
Victim and victor both be damned.
Eyes that see two sides of the coin,
Through the ether, we are all conjoined,
And live and love and die as one,
Burning in the brilliant wisdom of the sun.

Flesh & Bone

Cut his skin and he'll bleed red,
Stab his heart and he'll be dead.
Kiss his lips and he will blush,
Strike him and tears he will shed,
Caress him and his face will flush.
He's just another man,
He's just another man.
Nothing more or less than,
He's just another man.

The Cliché Touché

Sometimes you wake up,
On the wrong side of the bed.
And when it comes to love,
It's your heels over your head.
Get ready for the time of your life,
Because, oh boy howdy, how time flies.
When the cat's got you tongue,
And you read between the lines.
You see that all that glitters isn't gold,
Once you're as old as the hills.
Don't get your panties in a wad,
Instead have nerves of steel.
Be brave as a lion, weak as a kitten,
And positively ugly as sin.
Shrug it off and you will find,
That laughter is the best medicine.

[continued]

[The Cliché Touché-continued]

It's all for one and one for all,
And see there's the writing on the wall.
You need to kiss and make up,
To discover the diamonds in the rough.
Only time will ever tell,
But trust me when I say,
"All's well that ends well."
Opposites attract and good looks will fade,
So when life gives you lemons,
Make some lemonade.

Beyond the Limits

Within this vessel of flesh and bone we dwell,
A symphony of limits, a fragile shell.
Through strength and frailty, we strive and
endure,
Bound by mortal bounds, our spirits assure.

Yet, yearning to transcend, we dare to dream,
To test the boundaries, explore the extreme.
Infinite horizons beckon us to roam,
But finite are the limbs that carry us home.

Our senses, marvels, glimpse the world's
facade,
Yet falter in capturing all that's wonderfully
made.
Eyes tire of beholding, ears crave new sound,
As we seek to grasp what cannot be found.

[continued]

[Beyond Limits-continued]

The body's strength ebbs, a temporal guise,
Aches and fatigue, where limitations lie.
Though muscles may weaken, spirits take
flight,
Defying boundaries, soaring through the
night.

For while our bodies may falter and decline,
The human spirit knows no final line.
We reach beyond, embracing the unknown,
Transcending the limits, in heart and in bone.

In unity of soul and flesh we find,
A resilience that defies these mortal confines.
So let us embrace our bodies' constraints,
For in their limitations, true strength remains.

<u>*Scurry*</u>

Beetles beetles, come out and play,
The summer sun has gone away,
And now that winter's bitter cold,
And all the glitters have gotten old,
We scurry fast across the floor,
Sneak through the windows and the door.
Nibble bits of trash and cheese,
And roam about just as we please,
Then revolting human turns on the light.
We panic, flee! Quick! Take flight,
But crash upon the cold clear glass,
Darkness descends. Fading fast…

The Lurking Man

If you see the Lurking Man,
Best to let him be,
For if he sees you seeing him,
Oh, what a fright he'll be!

The Lurking Man is always near,
And rarely makes a sound.
Do your best to ignore him,
Or else you'll wake up underground.

Have you seen the Lurking Man,
A shadow in your eye?
Spider limbs that shake and charge.
How he loves to make you cry.

What Comes with the Rain

Raindrops dance upon the glass,
A surrealist symphony, bizarre and vast.
Clocks melt, and time warps in fluid streams,
As reality dissolves into fragmented dreams.

Umbrellas sprout wings and take flight,
Carrying souls to mystical heights.
Fish swim through the aqueous air,
While upside-down trees sprout roots in
despair.

Raindrops whisper secrets in hushed tones,
Revealing tales of forgotten stones.
Electric skies crackle with vibrant hues,
As surreal visions blur the world's views.

[continued]

[What Comes with the Rain-continued]

Windows become portals to ethereal realms,
Where unicorns roam and sirens overwhelm.
In this watery world of endless surprise,
Gravity loses grip, and imagination flies.

The rain outside the window unfolds a show,
Where fantasy reigns and logic must go.
Embrace the absurdity, let your mind roam
free,
In this mystical downpour, escape from
reality.

Midnight

Owl silent sentry,
Owl watching over me.
The moon an apple skin-bare,
Into my soul's depth he stares.

Raw and cautious and optimistic,
In the darkness life is so simplistic.
Slips like a ghost across dead bones,
It sings, it whispers, hollow moans.

Monsters frolic, goblins play,
Freed at last from the day.
Couldn't escape from the dream,
Mouth wide open, empty scream.

Walk the moors, haunt the halls,
Mind numb memories I can't recall.
Falls from the mountain dark midnight,
Embraced by radiant haunted starlight.

Storm Cloud

When the rain pitter-patters,
And the howling wind blows,
You wonder what sort of storm cloud,
Has begun to grow.
Leaves fall to the sound,
Of the thunder's boom,
And the walls shake and tremble,
Inside of every room.

Was that a bit of lighting,
Flashing in the night?
There for a moment,
And then gone from our sight.
The air hisses and rumbles,
With angry shouts.
A beckoning taunt,
"Come out. Come out."

[continued]

[Storm Cloud-continued]

Cower in the closet,
Hiding deep inside.
You wonder of the ocean,
And it's rising tides.
And how the earth does tremble.
Oh, mercy how it quakes!
And forest and fields of kindling,
Just ready to be baked.

There simply is no stopping,
The swirling angry storm.
There's only just to hide,
And shelter when they warn.
Stormy weather's brewing,
The kettle's piping hot,
Stormy weather's coming,
Wheater you're ready or you're not.

<u>The Old Oak Tree</u>

Let us go,
To the old oak tree,
And the witchy woman,
Will spin a tale for me.
With a shiny penny,
We'll pay her fee.
Come let us go,
To the old oak tree.

I see it now,
The old oak tree.
With burning bonfire,
And summer smoked brandy.
We'll dance with the witchy woman,
And she'll spin a tale for me,
Yes, I can see it now,
The old oak tree.

[continued]

[The Old Oak Tree-continued]

Go and sit under,
The old oak tree.
As shadows arrive,
And buzz like the bees.
The witchy woman smiles,
Oh, she's got a tale for me.
So gladly do I pay her her fee,
Underneath that old oak tree.

I left it there,
Underneath the old oak tree.
With the witchy woamn,
And her shiny penny fee.
She told me a tale,
Crafted just for me,
And I buried it there,
Beneath the old oak tree.

My Head and My Heart

Logic dictates caution, to guard and protect,
To shield my heart from the pain and regret,
But emotions surge, like a tumultuous sea,
My heart insists, "This is love, so let it be."

My head speaks of reason, of practicality,
To weigh the pros and cons, with clarity,
Yet my heart dances freely, like a soaring
dove,
Whispering softly, "Oh, but this is love."

The mind seeks answers, to analyze and
compare,
To navigate the complexities, the risks we
must bear,
Yet the heart speaks a language only it can
tell,
"Embrace the unknown, for love knows it
well."

[continued]

[My Head and My Heart-continued]

Reason may argue, with facts and with sense,
But love is an emotion, defying all pretense,
It sweeps us away, like a gentle, sweet breeze,
Whispering, "Stay here, for love brings such
peace."

Conflicting desires, a battle deep within,
To follow the mind or to let the heart win,
But deep in my soul, a truth rises above,
This isn't some fairytale, this never was love.

Foes Make the Best Friends

I have a funny friend,
He's always mad at me,
We tend to jest and joke about,
But he often doesn't see,
What wisdom does the ditch weed,
Say to the tall oak tree,
When it comes to talk of dogs and dames,
The birds and the bees,
The battle of wits often ends,
With an, "Agree to disagree,"
It easy enough to misunderstand,
Mistake us for being enemies,
We can quickly stab the other,
Then invite him out for tea,
Some may compare out bond,
To a paddle boat at sea,
But truthfully we just don't know,
Of any other way to be,
It's hard to explain how,
To spar fills us with such glee,

[continued]

[Foes Make the Best Friends-continued]

When we fondly recall times,
With beastly beautiful banshees,
Or better still memories,
Of all the trouble we had to flee,
And so I shall make this vow,
A cursed damned decree,
Surround yourself with people,
That make you question what you see.

The most powerful thing you can be is a memory.

APRIL

<u>*Season's Greeting*</u>

Butterflies all fly away,
Beyond the setting sun, pass the light of day.
If heaven only knows, the secrets that we tell,
I wish them all the better, indeed I wish them well.
Sparrows soar in with the spring,
Summer clinging to their wings.
Of dew grass shimmering gold,
A peaceful land is what I'm told.
Where lilies like to whisper, and frogs bellow out their call.
Perhaps we'll meet again, in the crossing of the fall.

<u>Infinity</u>

Moon drunk on stars. Moon drunk on
madness.
All the *"What if?"*'s, they fill me with sadness.
Waterfall labyrinth mutes the whispers,
But don't once dare to disturb.

The clock workers tick tick tick time away,
Blind to the meaning of a year, of a day.
Lost in the bliss would be a dream,
But I can not abandon all that I've seen.

Whatever the outcome, whatever the score,
I will dance blindly on the broken shores.
What is a memory that's not yet mine?
What is a moment, but a breath of time?

Drowning

Screaming eyes,
Reach out to me,
As the body drifts away.
I'm frozen.
Nay, I'm paralyzed,
By what my own eyes say.

A dead man floating,
Who isn't yet dead,
But trapped inside his corpse.
Left to rot, left to die,
All the while still alive,
For this is hell and at its worst.

Fight the water,
Break the tides,
Carefully take him in my arms.
Swim to shore,
Call for help,
But the river's done its harm.

I wish I said "I love you" more,
But now it's much too late.
I wish I told you how you made me laugh,
But regret is to be my fate.
If I had just another day,
Even an hour with you dear,
I'd tell you all the things,
That I had wanted you to hear.

I'd tell you of the future,
That you never got to see.
I'd tell you of these new memories,
That you should have shared with me.
If Death could be so giving,
As to give me a moment more,
I'd scoop you up and hold you tight,
As we stood along dark shores.

[continued]

[Wish Upon a Star-continued]

Looking back on yesterdays,
Is a path to lightly tread.
For you are gone and I can't wait,
Wasting time off in my own head.
There is still some life left,
That I must go and live.
Some laughter and some love,
That I must go and give.

I wished I said, "I love you," more,
But now you are long gone,
I wish I'd let you know then,
How important was our bond.
You're off skipping rocks on rain clouds,
While we're here splashing in the mud.
My only hope and prayer my dear,
Is that you know that you were loved.

Farewell

In the depths of the night, a whispered sigh,
Unspoken words that haunt the sky.
Regrets like echoes, they amplify,
"I didn't get a chance to say goodbye,"

Time slipped away, too swift and sly,
Leaving empty spaces, and tears to dry.
Unanswered questions, reasons why,
"I didn't get a chance to say goodbye,"

The memories linger, like a gentle cry,
Of cherished moments, now held awry.
Unfinished chapters, a heartfelt sigh,
"I didn't get the chance to say goodbye,"

And in the depths of sorrow, hope shall lie,
An eternal bond that never will die.
I watch the sunset, and burning ships fly,
"I didn't get the chance to tell you goodbye."

Fades Away

Washes over me like rain. Drenches me to the
bone.
Land. Life. Lover. Is there nothing that's my
own?
Eternity where are you? Just a shadow of the
day.
Mystery surrender as fair uncertainty likes to
play.

Dashed against the blooming dawn.
Dashed against the reckless wind.
What once stood proud upon the stone,
Crumbles now, we can't defend.

Race towards it now,
And hold it tight,
And dare not let it go.
Beware the fickle weathered time,
For never do you know.

What's here today may soon be gone,
Like the blinking of an eye.
So, hold it deep, just like a breath,
That vanishes with a sigh.

Life is just one grand bouquet of many
moments past,
Red roses for all the lovers, who never seemed
to last.
Daisys of April's cheer, a spring that's gone
astray,
For tiny little blossoms, will bless the month
of May.

And Primrose for devotion, as wedding bells
do chime.
Daffodil for my fresh start, if you'll forgive my
crimes.
With loyalty, my dear Carnation will stoically
soldier on,
But Lily of the Valley will sing her bitter
funeral song.

[continued]

[Bouquet of Life-continued]

May the Poppies bring me strength, as Aster
gives me valor,
For there seems to be a perfect flower, for each
and every hour.
It seems a silly thing, to mark these days gone
by,
Yet just the same as a wilting flower, softly
away time flies.

Dancer

It dances in on the heels of winter,
Brushes snow from off of sleeping eyes.
It is like waking from a dream and stretching,
And finding the loveliest of surprises.

It's come again, just as it did the year before.
Playfully frolicking through hills and fields,
But blows again, vengeful winter,
Yet the youngster doesn't yield.

Instead, it waits 'til winter's winded,
And picks up its dance once more.
For no matter how cold things may get,
Spring will come again for sure.

<u>Dark Waters</u>

Bubbles burst and mermaids sink,
And darkness floats all around.
Down in the depth waits something,
That lurks without a sound.

Chilled corpse cold and still,
Chops the waves up and down.
Beneath the surface, quiet, still,
Something lurks without a sound.

It's closing in, you can't escape.
Careful, before you're found.
Creature made in Hunger's shape,
Lurks behind you, without a sound.

The West Wind

Blow Tallahassee, blow,
Rattle those devil bones.
Sing the witch's song.
Tell them all I ain't comin' home.

The soup bird's gone down south now,
And the cricket's in the bed out cold.
Lord Boy never had a chance now,
Blow Tallahassee, blow.

Went to fetch my iron,
Went to fetch my coal.
Got caught by a spotted viper,
Oh, blow Tallahassee, blow.

Sunk sinner's deep in the mud,
They dragged me something low.
That old sapling's where I'm hung,
Singing blow Tallahassee, blow.

<u>*Love's Fading Flame*</u>

In the vast expanse of time's embrace,
A truth emerges, steadfast and clever.
With each passing moment, we come to know,
That in this world, nothing lasts forever.

The golden sun, it dances in the sky,
But even its radiance will fade away.
For day turns to night, and night turns to day,
A cycle of change, where nothing can stay.

The flowers bloom, their petals so vibrant,
Yet they wither, succumbing to the earth's
call.
Their beauty, ephemeral, like a fleeting dream,
Reminding us that nothing can stand forever
tall.

[continued]

[Love's Fading Flame-continued]

So let us cherish the moments we hold dear,
Embrace the fleeting joys that grace our way.
For in the impermanence, life finds its grace,
And teaches us the art of living each and every
day.

For in this ever-changing tapestry of existence,
We find solace in the truth we uncover.
In every beginning, in evey ending,
We find that nothing lasts forever.

<u>***Flower on the Hill***</u>

To be a flower,
For just an hour,
Would be such a marvelous thing.
I could sit in the sun,
Speak to no one,
Dressed in the melody of Spring.

There'd be no worries,
Except winter flurries,
But the cold is so very far away.
To be a flower,
For just an hour,
Perfectly free in every way.

No cautions to heed,
Oh yes indeed,
I think right here I'll stay.

This Too Shall Pass

What couldn't stay we'll keep in our dreams,
We'll hold it tight and fuel it with screams.
And the doors that closed, we'll keep them
closed,
Hide away from the truth, bitter and cold.
Instead, we'll clutch to memories unyielding,
Lie and paint ourselves like stones unfeeling.
Head held high, and eyes shut tight,
We'll soldier on, headfirst into the fight.
Hearts will home the hunger and hurt,
With the lines of rise and ruin we will flirt.
The past fades with the pagans of the wind,
All things that begin, will all someday end.

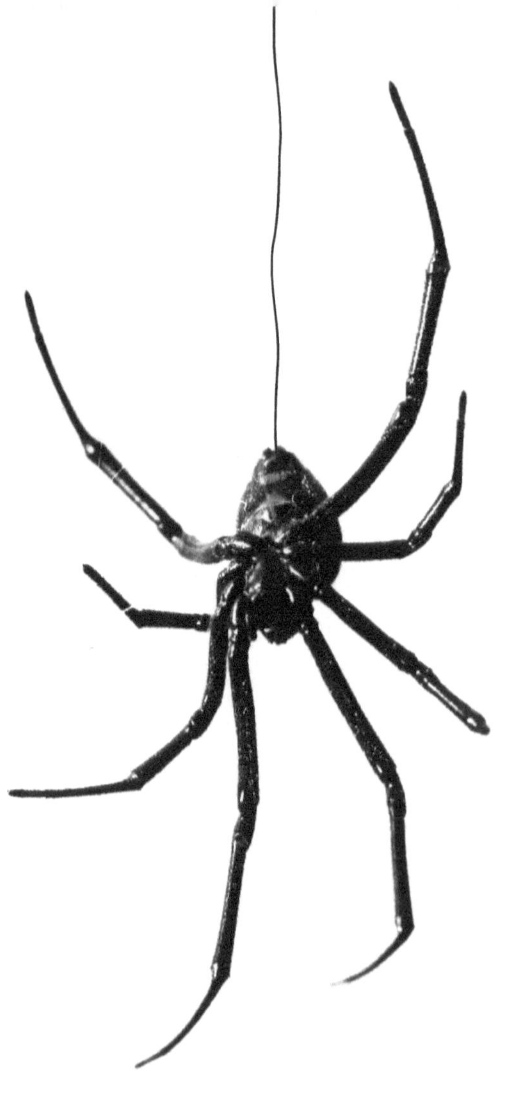

Pain is the magic that summons monsters.

MAY

<u>Dare to Be Stupid</u>

Dare to be stupid, let go of the norm,
Challenge the boundaries, weather the storm,
Only the foolish find treasures untold,
By venturing into the unknown bold.

To be silly, absurd, a playful buffoon,
Is to dance with life's whims, like a sweet tune,
For in laughter's embrace, the soul takes
flight,
And burdens dissolve, as day turns to night.

Embrace the jesters, the clowns, and the fools,
Unleash your spirit, defy all the rules,
Dare to be stupid, let your heart run free,
In the realm of possibilities, see what could be.

Dare to be stupid, defy expectations,
Embrace the joy of spontaneous creations,
For in the realm of foolishness, you'll find,
A world of wonder that expands the mind.

A Soul Set Free

As the universe blossoms and stars grow,
The moon speaks less than she knows.
Between the whispers one can hear,
And with this knowing, she grows each year.
Until the ringing bell at last sets free,
For none do dare define me.

A wilting lily drenched in dew,
Like I with memories of you.
To which the toil not meant to last,
When passed we say went to fast.
Away I go to dance with bees,
And none do dare deny me.

Into battle of monsters and men,
They discover that this will won't bend.
Onward I go, into the unknown,
Like crashing rivers demand to flow.
I am the storm upon the sea,
None shall dare to defy me.

The Witchy Woman

There lives a witchy woman,
Just beyond the hill,
They say she's mighty evil,
With a temper that could kill.

She drinks expensive whiskey,
And dances naked in the night,
She speaks without a single care,
And gives the folks such a fright.

Beware the witchy woman,
Is what the old ones always say,
Her spirit is a thunderstorm,
But her face is pretty as the day.

She need no man to manage her,
Nor babes over which to fuss,
She spends her days just as she pleases,
And never feeling rushed.

Yes, there lives a witchy woman,
And they tell us to take heed,
Best we are to fall in line,
Or else another witchy woman you might be.

<u>*The Hunger*</u>

Have you ever felt the hunger,
Like claws upon your skin?
Have you ever tasted the thirst,
That burns you from within?

It's rare to find it in this day,
Of painted apathetic numbness.
The consuming feasting fiend,
Makes the mind obsessed.

To feel it is both equal parts,
The purest bliss and cruelest hell.
Have you ever felt the hunger?
Come sit with me and tell.

The Rain

The rain sounds like sorrow,
The rain sounds like Spring,
The rain sounds like memories,
And half-forgotten things.

The rain brings me peace.
It pauses all time.
And there, for a moment,
I'm free of all my crimes.

I'm free of the sights,
I'm free of the sounds,
I'm free of the world,
When the rain comes around.

The Wisdom of Children

Sleepy little children, sink deep into dreams.
What marvelous minds, such whimsical things.
Small creatures of light and confusion and
trust.
Blind to the world in their eager rush.

Laughter, cries, and babbling sounds.
Such infinite potential, the universe unbound.
The beauty of all for they see with their hearts.
The power of innocence, sharp as a dart.

Tranquil little goblins, perfect little trolls.
They are living nostalgia, that is their role.
To remind us all of a far simpler time,
Of forts and hugs and nursery rhymes.

Damn Girl

It's no secret, that passion burning in your
heart,
Light up that inferno, love hard but play
smart.
It's not easy, this path that you walk,
All the lies and the whispers, oh how they
mock.

Damn girl, dry your eyes,
I promise you everything's gonna be alright.
Damn girl, why is life not fair,
When you give them your heart and they don't
even care.
Damn girl, when you just can't win,
Stand your ground and try, try, try again.

It wasn't love, that tore you in two,
It wasn't love that left you black and blue,
Trust me, when the whole world falls apart,
You can pick up the pieces of your broken
heart.
Wash away all of your sorrows and bitterness,
And try not to listen when they paint you as
villainous.

Never Surrender

The taste of blood and dirt,
The sting of the fall and hurt,
My feet fumble but find the ground,
And I stand up for another round.

The laughter that slaps across the face,
Tripping at the very start of the race,
So tempting to lie there and call it the end,
But I do not break, no matter how much I
bend.

The storm clouds that loom,
The darkness that blooms,
A swirling madness that gives me a fright,
Yet somehow, I know, it'll all be alright.

The Angel with the Broken Wings

What good are these broken wings to me?
A reminder of dreams that may never be,
Once I believed I could conquer the skies,
But now I'm grounded, unable to rise.

What good are these feathers, tattered and
torn?
In a world that expects me to soar and adorn,
In the depths of despair, I question my fate,
With broken wings, burdened by their weight.

Oh, how I yearn to reach for the heights,
But these broken wings are my endless plight.
What good are these broken wings to me?
A reminder of dreams that never shall be.

<u>*Said Is Dead*</u>

I never cared so much for words easily spoken,
easily shed,
And so, I say, and believe it true, for me all
that is said is dead.
Instead, let me see what narrow path a person
treads,
For action speaks louder than voices, a poetry
easily read.
It's not an easy task for some, the heart tries to
fool the head,
The ear gorges on cunning lies when loneliness
needs fed,
And in a whirlwind one flows into another,
like a wildfire spreads.
Then reality breaks the words to shards, and
soon they cut and shred.
A person can die waiting for words that will
soothe all of their dread,
Not thinking once, or even twice, that it was
for words that they bled,
And out spills sorrow, pain and grief, the most
ravenous of reds.
And so, I say once more to you, I say that said
is dead!

<u>*Let the Children Light the Way*</u>

Teach your children all that you wished you
had known,
Unleash the wisdom within you, like seeds to
be sown.
Let your voice guide them, like a beacon in the
night,
Illuminate their path, with love as their
guiding light.

Share the lessons learned from the battles
you've fought,
The mistakes that shaped you, the wisdom
they bought.
Nurture their hearts with empathy and care,
Instill in them the values you hold dear and
rare.

Teach them kindness, compassion, and grace,
To embrace diversity and never judge by face.
Empower their minds, let curiosity bloom,
Encourage their dreams, let their spirits
consume.

[continued]

[Let the Children Light the Way-continued]

Show them the strength in vulnerability's
embrace,
To seek understanding and stand in someone
else's place.
Inspire their dreams, ignite their passions
ablaze,
Guide them to believe, that they hold power to
amaze.

Teach your children resilience in the face of
defeat,
To rise from failure, with courage, they'll
meet.
Impart the value of integrity, in actions big
and small,
To walk with honor and dignity, standing tall.

Teach them to chase their dreams, with ardor
and zest,
To never settle for less, to always give it their
best.
Instill in them the power of love's unyielding
might,
To be a beacon of hope, in a world so filled
with plight.

Curse of Fire

I ran so far from the fires I had set with my
own hands.
The echoes of my mistakes across desolate
lands.
In shadows deep, where remorse does reside,
A trail of destruction, flames flickering wide.

The embers of guilt, they whispered and
burned,
Regret etched deep, lessons harshly learned.
As I sought solace in darkness, where demons
reside,
In the wreckage I created, I could no longer
hide.

I fled from the inferno, my heart heavy with
shame,
A tangled web of choices, too late to reclaim.
Knowing the havoc I caused, the pain I
unleashed,
And so was born the evil dragon, the fiery
beast.

Blessing

Bless the way my feet shuffle,
And bless the way that they dance.
Bless the storms that wash over me,
And all the horrors that entrance.

Bless the messes, mistakes, misgivings.
Bless the monster and the man.
Bless the darkness looming.
Bless the cowards that all ran.

Bless the wounds that heal us.
Bless the pain that makes us grow.
Bless the demons and the darkness.
Grant them the compassion we are shown.

For all the prophets and the poets, for the liars and the cheats, we're all in this mess together, ain't life a funny little thing.

JUNE

<u>***Yeah, But You Didn't***</u>

"I could do that," but you did not,
This is just another person's poisonous brain
rot.
People scoffing just because they "could",
Well then, darling, let me tell you what you
should.

You should pick a pen, a brush,
Or perhaps an original thought.
You should run with risk and failure,
Until some inspiration's caught.

You could do that? Why yes you could!
And yet you never will…
Now it's time that you understood,
Before I stab you with my quill.

<u>***Blue***</u>

I looked around all the world,
And all I saw was blue.
The sky, the sea,
The eyes staring at me.
From up above to down below,
Blue, blue, crystal cold.

I ventured far across the desert blue,
Splashed with pigments of morning dew,
And just as I feared, there or here,
All the world surrounded by blue.

Blue skies, blue eyes, blue lips that lie.
Blue hands upon a blue chest.
A blue heart in a cold breast.
Blue, blue, blue.

It flooded in, it filled me up,
Like a drink spilling from my cup.
Blue that haunts, blue that sings,
Blue tormented chilling thing.

<u>*Anxiety*</u>

I stand alone in the crowd,
Hear them speak, hear them laugh.
I open my mouth to join despite my doubt,
Open my mouth but no sound comes out.
Wave my hands, but no one sees,
I'm nothing more than a blowing breeze.

I stand alone in the crowd,
With people gathered all around.
I feel so lost, I feel so cold,
Like I've forgotten the lines I'm supposed to know.
Force a smile, fake a laugh,
And pray the moment passes fast.

I stand alone in the crowd,
My heart, it hammers far too loud.
Stomach rolls, twists in knots,
Like a rabbit, trapped and caught.
Panic shivers, I can't escape,
From this living nightmare I wish to wake.

<u>Rotten Roger</u>

Flesh and bone, they rot away,
Laying here in the cold damp grave.
Misery, such sweet release,
Torment pure and deafening.
What fresh hell must I endure?
For the pain of Hell there is no cure.
The maggots creep and crawl down inside,
I feel them burrow into my eyes,
And skin shrivels up while fluids leak out.
I try to scream; I try to shout.
Meat slops off my haunted bones,
It matters not how grand my throne,
For all the same Death came for me.
It mattered not my victories.
Paralyzed as time drags on,
I hear only the grave's buzzing song.
Skeletal remains are all that I am,
Such is the life of one so damned.
The smell is wicked and plagues my soul.
The grave is cruel. Dark and cold.
I wish to do it all again!
I'd be a better man! I'd be a better friend!
At last, I fear it's much too late,
For here I rot in my prison grave.

The Gallows Walk

Remember,
Remember,
Always and forever,
You come up a little,
Before it all ends.

<u>*A is for Apple*</u>

A is for Apple, of which I have none,
B is for Beer, of which I've had some,
C is for Cash, so easily spent,
D is for Dog, and wherever the hell he went,
E is for Easy, just like Sally-Ann McCall,
F is for Frisky, which is also like Sally-Ann McCall,
G is for Green, which my thumbs are not,
H is for Herb, which is found in paper or pot,
I is for Iceland, they're whooping our ass,
J is for Jail, which I think I'll just pass,
K is for Kisses and L is for Lips,
M is for Mouth and N is for-
Noses! I was going to say Noses…
O is for the Opossum, I took out with my truck,
P is for the Possum, in my bumper he's stuck,
Q is for Quiet, I've had a long day,
R is for Randy, which is another word for play,

[continued]

[A is for Apple-continued]

S is for Secrets, you'll never know mine,
T is for Tales, that grow on the grapevines,
U is for Utah, and all of your wives,
V is for Vasectomy, best done with small
knives,
W is for Witches, and their magical power,
X is for X-rays, and reminds me of chemical
showers,
Y is for none other than the magnificent You,
Z is for none other than your home at the
Zoo.

<u>*What We Are*</u>

Pink and squishy lump of me,
I wonder wonder what you see.
When you look into a mirror,
Distorted visions oh so queer.

Oh, happy day it must be,
To truly know myself as me!
Is it so odd a thing to think,
We're all just lumps of squishy pink.

<u>***Scorch***</u>

Let us talk of poets darling,
Oh, let us speak of love.
Let us bathe in moonlight,
Just like the stars above.

Let me take your hand in mine,
And softly kiss your name.
Let me learn your magic ways,
Oh, let me play your games.

Let them talk and wonder,
Those that dare to do.
Let them have their world,
For all I need is you.

Let me dote and spoil you,
Until you're rotten to the core.
Let me charm and worship you,
Until you're begging out for more.

Let us not waste one moment,
On worrying about what's right.
Let us forget about all else,
Save for the beauty of the night.

You Were Warned

I told you not to get too close,
Trust me you were warned.
I promised you it'd end in tears,
That I would cause you harm.

Things started off all rosy,
I could tell that you'd been blind.
Not really seeing me for me,
I knew one day you'd find,

The darkness in my laughter,
The monster in my heart.
I told you not to love me.
I warned you from the start.

<u>***Midnight Poison***</u>

Midnight poison what have you done to me?
You've made me a poet. You've made me an enemy.
And what motive could you have,
To make such a fool of me.
Such rotten code of conduct,
Was that your victory?
And could you have perhaps,
Not made me slur so much.
And when tomorrow comes,
Please don't make such a fuss.

Off I Go

Shooting stars of emerald green,
Come racing down to catch a dream,
Of waves crashing against the shore,
That pounds and pounds, more and more,
Til rock gives way and crashes down,
Onto the fay all splashing 'round,
Splashing 'round now not so much,
Excited chaos, the others rush,
Make haste! Be quick, else there'll be nothing
left,
As the fay sinks deeper, losing breath,
A breath of fire that cuts and bleeds,
For Death is not so frightening,
Indeed, it is but a forgotten friend,
Who's come to greet us at the end,
And walk with us on down that path,
We talk and visit and give a laugh,
It was so silly, that life I had,
And I shall miss it, but don't feel sad,

[continued]

[Off I Go-continued]

For this life must end so I can be born anew,
A second chance at loving you,
Up into the sky I go,
On into the great unknown,
The nerves, they shake me to my core,
Like crashing waves against the shore,
Comes raining down an emerald green,
Shooting stars and forgotten dreams.

Within

You never seemed to understand,
That it was never about the curve of your face,
But rather the gentle deeds of your hands,
For that, my darling, was your grace.

It was never about the skin you wore,
But the poetry inside your heart.
Your value is not some aesthetic score,
But your wit as sharp as any dart.

You never need to hide from me,
Fearing I shall ever judge mere looks.
Instead let me drown in the depths of you,
Consumed not by the cover but by the book.

With me feel free to dance and sing,
And be as perfectly you as you can be.
Know that what I seek is a hidden thing,
And know that your beauty never scared me.

<u>***Undone***</u>

Baby born so perfect,
Despite my crying lungs,
Little bundle to protect,
But I wasn't done.

And through the years I got better,
So clever are the young,
I was the guide by which to measure,
And yet I wasn't done.

Of facts and finds I filled my head,
To climb the highest, the greatest fun,
I drank in all that I read,
But no, I wasn't done.

Sometimes I tumbled, tripped and fell,
And oh, how that failure of mine stung,
I'd strive and sweat to leave that hell,
Because I wasn't done.

And though I grew gray and somewhat old,
I never stopped to hold my tongue,
I could live eons still, and Death will be told,
"Oh! But I'm not done!"

JULY

<u>***Dare***</u>

Be a disappointment. A heartbreak. A
mistake.
Better to live wounded, than die from the
ache.
That aching, bleeding, beating call to action,
So demanding, and yet, so out of fashion.

Dare to stumble, to trip, to fall and fail,
Damn the odds, dare to risk, set sail.
Live your life with your heart at ease.
When it comes to dreams, do as you please.

There is no second chances here, Love,
So be a disappointment, reach for the stars
above.
There is no going back, can never hit rewind,
So dare to be bold and dare to be kind.

The Wisdom of Youth

When you are young, they assume you know
nothing,
A world of mysteries unfolds before your eyes.
They underestimate your capacity to grow,
To learn, to explore, to reach for the skies.

But within your heart, a fire burns bright,
Curiosity and wonder fuel your eager mind.
You question, you seek, you hunger for
knowledge,
A thirst for understanding that's one of a kind.

They may dismiss your ideas as mere child's
play,
But you hold a wisdom they fail to perceive.
For in your innocence lies a spark of truth,
Untarnished by the biases that they believe.

So let their assumptions be the wind at your
back,
Fuel for the journey, to forge a path instead
Prove to the world that youth holds the power,
To reshape, to inspire, to face what's ahead.

Now

Things I often can't remember,
Are the words I meant to say.
There's no promise of tomorrow,
There's no return to yesterday.

Eyes and windows can not hide,
And if what they say is true,
We only have this moment now,
A moment here with you.

So give it everything you've got,
Don't hold back one second more.
It's time to let the lion out,
And let them hear you roar.

<u>Forever Always</u>

Fear not little Dove, I'll hold your hand.
I know this big world is hard to understand.
I'll walk beside you and hold you tight.
So do not worry in the dark of night.

Fret not little Blossom, I am right here.
My heart is yours, even when I'm not near.
The booming storm, the rippling rain,
I'll do my best to shield you from pain.

Fuss not little Willow, I'll wait and listen,
As you grow and change, through all life's
transitions.
When this world is so twisted, and things get
alarming.
Trust that I'll try to understand you my
darling.

Forget not little Lambs, I am yours for-
always.
Every minute, of every hour, of every day.
As certain as the sun, and the wind, and the
sky,
I'll love you forever. Forever, always.

May we raise difficult children, strong and bold,
With curious minds that never cease to ask, "Why?"
May they stumble and falter, their paths unfold,
Yet rise with resilience, wipe the tears from their eyes.

Let them taste failure, the bitter and the sweet,
For in each mistake, lessons they shall find.
May they face challenges, no fear of defeat,
And rise again, stronger, with a steadfast mind.

May they wander through uncertainty's haze,
Exploring the depths of their own desires.
With every stumble, they'll learn life's maze,
Finding courage within, fueling their inner fires.

[continued]

[Footprints of the Future-continued]

Let them experience the ache of their mistakes,
Embrace the lessons learned from each fall.
With tears wiped away, may their spirit
awake,
Ready to face the world, standing tall.

For it's in the journey of struggle and strife,
That character is forged, resilience takes its
flight.
May they embody strength in the face of life,
With heads held high, shining with inner light.

So let us raise difficult children with pride,
Knowing they'll face the world with hearts
aglow,
In their journey, they'll trip, but never hide,
For they'll rise up again and their spirits will
grow.

<u>*Opportunity*</u>

Golden opportunity, slippery as they come,
Best hold tight, like sand through fingers it
runs.

And they say it's all simply a blessin' or a
lesson,
But it's a lesson that is the bitterest to learn.
Taunting 'What if's that keep you guessing,
While the truth of reality bites and burns.

Second chances are gifted, but never
guaranteed.
Do all you can while you can, for regret's a
bastard breed.

<u>*Sharks*</u>

Thicker than water. Draws you in.
Razor jaws. Hope you can swim.
Fast as lightning. It's frightening.
It's coming for you. Angry and biting.

Below the surface, it patiently waits.
Drowning dark waters will be your fate.
It lurks inside that crystal blue.
Smells red and now it's after you.

Swim fast and just maybe you'll get away.
Survive to go swimming another day.
But the water's its world, and it's the king.
It drags you down, but it wasn't a dream.

<u>*Can't Break Me*</u>

In the face of trials, I stand tall and free,
For it takes more than you to break someone
like me.
Though winds may howl and storm clouds
loom,
I'll rise above, my spirit won't be consumed.

In the depths of darkness, I find my light,
A flame that flickers, but never loses sight.
Through battles fought and scars I bear,
I emerge stronger, with unwavering stare.

With every blow dealt, I grow resilient and
tough,
For within my core, strength is more than
enough.
The weight of adversity won't bring me down,
I'm a warrior, unyielding, wearing a victor's
crown.

[continued]

[Can't Break Me-continued]

Through the tempest's fury, I find my way,
Navigating the chaos, come what may.
I'll forge my path with courage and grit,
Defying the odds, I refuse to submit.

No, it takes more than you to break my spirit,
For I possess a fire that you can't inhibit.
I'll rise from the ashes, like a phoenix in flight,
With unwavering determination, I'll conquer
the fight.

So, bring your challenges, your tests, your
strife,
I'll overcome, for I am forged with life.
In the face of defeat, I'll always be,
An unbreakable force, forever strong, you see.

For within my soul, a resilience resides,
A spirit that endures, undeterred by tides.
Try as you might, but you'll never succeed,
For it takes more than you to break someone
like me.

Just

Do it not for your grandfather but for your
grandson,
Do it for those not yet here, not for the ones
already gone,
Do it for the masses, do it for the crowds,
Do it so one day you can make yourself
proud,
Do it because it's hard, do it because you can,
Do it because it's better than living life second
hand,
Do it even though the world may tell you no,
Do it because storms are how gardens grow,
Do it for those who never had a chance,
Do it because it makes your spirit dance,
Do it at noon and night, do it despite the rain,
Do it to feed that hunger inside, that gnaws
against your brain,
Do it for the heroes whose tales we never
heard,
Do it despite the voices that called what you
do absurd,
Do it not for fame and glory, nor for fake
friends you find,
Do it because it matters, like a haunting spirit
of the mind.

Dancehall of the Dead

The moon, it lights the way,
To the dancehall of the dead.
No need for invitation,
To the dancehall of the dead.

We slip through gates and doors,
To the dancehall of the dead.
We laugh and frolic merrily,
To the dancehall of the dead.

Spirits twist and turn,
Ghosts shimmy and they shake.
The music of the night,
Gives the living such a fright!

Come and join us here,
At the dancehall of the dead.

The Driftwood Man

I made myself a driftwood man,
One gray and lonely day.
They said a storm was blowing in,
But I decided I should stay.

He had a brittle bundle for a chest,
And his eyes were fishbone skulls.
He was rather tall and lanky,
And he had a horseshoe for a smile.

The wind it started howling,
I think it spoke his name.
For as the rain began to spill,
It seemed he had grown a brain.

And turned his head and moved his eyes,
And I stood there stunned stone still.
But the storm blew very hard that day,
Suppose I could build another…
Though I doubt I ever will.

Coming Down the Hill

Dead men tell no tales,
Dead men tell no tales.
Best to let them on their way.
Watch them as they go.
Those marching marching bones.
Dead men tell no tales.

Dead men tell no tales,
Dead men tell no tales.
All the secrets they won't say.
Oh, what they must have seen.
So terrible and mean.
Hope they don't take me.

Dead men tell no tales,
Dead men tell no tales.
Yet they've come again today.
What business brings them here?
When they look into the mirror,
Wonder what they see.

Dead men tell no tales,
So, I guess we'll never know.
Watch them as they go.
Those marching marching bones.

Jar of Happy

There sits a jar upon the shelf,
Of all my happy things.
Sunsets, roses, kitten noses,
And songs that bluebirds sing.

Of all that lives inside that jar,
I drink sweet nectar of blissful joy.
For when I'm feeling a bit pulled down,
My jar of happy I do deploy.

There's many other kinds and ways,
To brighten up one's frigid days.
Yet I have found that, at least for me,
A jar of happy is all I need.

And what happiness inside resides!
Piano keys and sparkling eyes,
And candies sweet, and hugs so warm.
I delight in Happiness's many forms.

AUGUST

For Greta

The sky is on fire,
And so am I.

It doesn't really matter why.
Soon enough we'll both die.
Pity we can't even say we tried.

With hit for hit and eye for eye,
No wonder now the world's deep fried.
Best take a moment and say your goodbyes.

To laugh and love and even cry.
We had our chance and now we fly.

The sky is on fire,
And now so am I.

My Gift to You

May you live in interesting times,
Where chaos reigns and peace declines,
May the whirlwind of fate twist your path,
A turbulent journey, filled with aftermath.

May you come to the attention of those in
authority,
Their watchful eyes fixed upon your entirety,
A target of scrutiny, under their watchful gaze,
Bound by their power, trapped in their maze.

May the gods give you everything you ever
asked for,
Desires fulfilled, yet leaving you craving for
more,
A hollow existence, drowning in material gain,
A life of abundance, plagued by inner pain.

[continued]

[My Gift to You-continued]

May every step you take be on wet sand,
Unstable ground, shifting beneath your
command,
With each stride, your footing uncertain,
A dance of instability, a constant burden.

And in the end, may history remember your
name,
Etched in infamy, a legacy of shame,
A cautionary tale, a warning to behold,
A life consumed by darkness, untold.

These curses I bestow, with venomous might,
May they haunt your days, may they plague
your nights,
May they linger, relentless, and never wane,
A reminder of the choices, the consequences,
your bane.

<u>**The Games We Play**</u>

A comedy,
A tragedy,
A romance,
All rolled into one.
These are the games we play with each other,
But only the monsters have fun.

Try to change our nature,
Try to even the score,
Try to love one another,
Try to do a little more.

We are all addicted to the havoc,
We are the ones with the twisted grins,
We are all creatures of habit,
And so it will end as it begins.

The Desperate Escape

Black stripe. White stripe.
I'm sorry. I need a favor.
I know it's been a long time,
But I'm desperate and need a savior.

This world, I'm drowning in it.
I'm lost. So much I don't understand.
They wonder how I could be this way.
I wonder how they can make demands.

Where were they when I was broken?
Where were they when I was bleeding?
When the door closed and smiles turned off,
Did they know the monster and its deeds?

Was it a blind eye that brought me here?
Was it a matter of out of sight out of mind?
They look at my desperation and call me a
monster.
If that's true, then I pray that I'm the only
one.

Davy's Drinking Song

Oh, we'll,
Drink, and drink, and drink, and drink,
Until there's nothing left.

Yes, we'll,
Drink, and drink, and drink, and drink,
Until we're out of breath.

Just,
Drink, and drink, and drink, and drink,
Until there's nothing more.

Yes,
Drink, and drink, and drink, and drink,
'Til we end up on the floor.

Gonna,
Drink, and drink, and drink, and drink,
'Til yesterday is gone.

[continued]

Yep, just,
Drink, and drink, and drink, and drink,
That is the business of this song.

So,
Drink, and drink, and drink, and drink,
'Til we've all run out of beer.

And then,
Drink, and drink, and drink, and drink,
And we'll be out of here!

<u>*Seven Singing Sailors*</u>

Seven singing sailors,
Set out to sea one day.
What happened on those tides,
No one can really say.

Seven singing sailors,
Dreaming pockets full f gold.
Went in search of riches,
At least that's what I'm told.

Seven singing sailors,
Found fortune, fame, and grinned.
They did not realize,
That their luck was about to spin.

Seven singing sailors,
Never returned from where they'd gone.
But if you listen closely,
You'll hear their sailors' song.

<u>***Come to Me***</u>

Burns and sweats but so delicious, this liberal
heat.
Blisters, swelts, but so addictive, this
forbidden treat.
It doesn't bundle up and hide, nor does it
quiver in the cold.
It comes bursting in, a foe, a friend, either way
I'm sold.

Dances naked in the street without a care or
shame.
Will kiss you on the lips, until you're begging
for its name.
But no name will it give, instead it madly runs
away.
Is this intoxicating vision going, or has it come
to stay?

[continued]

[Come to Me-continued]

Like a drunken lover, you know you shouldn't
go to.
It's blinding with its sudden beauty, rich and
crystal blue.
The heat it burns so pleasantly, dressed just in
dirty sweat,
And just as you've learned its madness, cold
fills you with regret.

<u>*Promises*</u>

Please forgive me, darling, know that it will all
be okay,
Please forgive me, darling, know if it were up
to me I'd stay.
And drink the heavenly waters of your lips,
Whisper dreams of forever as time slowly
ticks.
We'd sail to paradise, we'd soar to the highest
heights,
We'd survive every bloody battle; we'd never
give up the fight.

So please forgive me, darling, for letting them
take me away.
Please forgive me, darling, I promise that it
will all be okay.
Try not to be too angry, try not to dwell on
life's cruel treachery.
Instead, promise me, my darling, that I'll live
forever in your memory.

[continued]

[Promises-continued]

Like the flash of lightning in the storm, like
the crack of the gunshot.
One moment we're walking the gold streets of
heaven, and the next second we're not.
Like the snap of a whip, the world shifts on a
dime,
And what was us yesterday is now a whole
lifetime away.
Couldn't keep all my promises, God knows I
tried.
Couldn't protect your smile, I never meant to
lie.

[continued]

[Promises-continued]

What was meant to be will someday find a
way,
And I know that it hurts right now, but I
promise this, promise this, that it'll all be
okay.
We're standing alone in the dark right now,
Terrified and hurt and desperate to be found.
Never thought for a moment our world could
ever change,
Never considered the possibility reality could
become so strange.
A minute without you is like a lifetime of hell,
But I'm standing and fighting, waiting for that
final bell.

[continued]

[Promises-continued]

Could never ever ever ever not be thinking
about you.
Could never ever ever ever stop longing for
you,
Your lips, your face, the touch of your skin,
your warm embrace.
If only I could just hold you right now,
If only I could return to yesterday, but I just
don't know how.

So please forgive me, my darling,
For letting them come and take me away.
So please forgive me, my darling,
I swear that one day it will all be okay.
Try not to cry for me, my darling,
Try to keep your head up and hold back your
tears.
Try not to be too angry,
Try not to surrender to your fears.
Instead promise this, promise this, my darling,
Try not to dwell on this bitter treachery.
Promise this, promise this, my darling,
That I'll live on in your memory.

Tell Me, Love

Tell me every terrible thing you ever did,
And let me love you anyways,
For I don't think I could ever love,
Someone who doesn't know how to
misbehave.

Share with me the stories you've kept hidden
in the dark,
The mistakes, the regrets, each and every
painful mark,
Tell me of the nights filled with foolish
escapades,
When ruffled rules were shattered and boring
boundaries frayed.

Reveal the secrets that burden your soul,
The moments of weakness that took their toll.
Let me be the one who sees your true face,
The scars, the bruises, each fall from grace.

<u>***What Could Have Been***</u>

It should have been you, it should have been
me,
It should have been all that we hoped and
dreamed.
It should have been love, it should have been
fate,
It should have been us, but we were just a little
too late.

And promises don't mean a damn when you
don't make the time,
And promises don't mean a damn when you
haven't got a dime.

So, let's fall back into the memories,
Of you and me.
Let's waste a moment,
Living in our forgotten dreams.

[continued]

[What Could Have Been-continued]

It should have been easy to say all that we
never said,
We should have followed our hearts and not
our stupid heads.
It should have been hard that day we said
goodbye,
Now that I think of it, did we ever really try?

And promises don't mean a damn when you're
not here,
And promises don't mean a damn when gone
are all the years.

You can't go back,
Life moves on.
Dreaming of you,
It's like poison siren songs.

All that we had has faded,
Life gets old and people grow jaded.
All that we were are now memories of,
Oh darling,
It should have been you,
It should have been me,
It should have been love.

<u>*Clock Runs Out*</u>

Of all the things I never knew,
The greatest of all was you.

Of all the places I'll never go,
The grandest of all would be your home.

Of all the people I never met,
It was for you that I had wept.

Of all the things that I did,
Time enough, life did not give.

<u>***Curfew Passes***</u>

We hide behind the iron gate,
We stand beneath the lamplight's glow.
Curfew has passed and we're so late.
The black car comes slowly down the road.

We huddle close together there,
And dare to only breathe in code.
For we can not even trust the air,
Ast the black car comes slowly down the road.

It's us and them and they're so strong.
Your courage, I wish it could be borrowed.
The end draws near as they creep along,
The black car comes slowly down the road.

[continued]

[Curfew Passes-continued]

I shut my eyes and hold them tight,
Hearing nothing but the echoing of toads.
The car has stopped, there's a flash of light,
Outside the black car has stopped along the road.

Snaps the gate, snaps the guard, snaps the gun.
My terror boils up and overflows.
We try to flee but we are outrun.
The black car speeds on down the road.

What a Mess Life Is

Looking at the mess I made,
From my first cry to the grave,
There's no catching perfection,
No keeping balance or counting score,
It's all the angle of perception.
The slaving and striving for something more.

The world could be a little greener,
Could do without getting any meaner,
I am beautiful mistakes and masterful chaos,
I am fragile, flaky, flippant, and foul.
A million treasures beyond cost.
A moon-drunk song the wild ones howl.

Could there be anything more absolute,
A better offering, a truer tribute,
The twisted knotted human world,
So much more and less than it seems,
Musical madness like you've never heard.
Brutal reality and waking dream.

SEPTEMBER

In the realm of honor and might,
Where cherry blossoms dance with light,
There lived a noble woman, strong and true,
The General's wife, with duties to pursue.

With her husband called off to distant lands,
To wield his sword and face war's demands,
She stood resolute, a beacon of grace,
Guiding their estate in his place.

The days turned to months, as time went by,
She tended to the lands, under their shared
sky,
A caretaker of abundance, fields so green,
Nurturing life, a serene and peaceful scene.

[continued]

[The General's Wife-continued]

But fate's cruel twist brought a storm to her
gate,
News of invaders, fueled by envy and hate,
With courage aflame, she rallied her might,
Prepared to defend, to stand and to fight.

She summoned her subjects, strong and true,
For they knew their loyalty, to her, was due,
Together they stood, a united band,
Ready to protect their cherished land.

With armor gleaming and swords held high,
They faced the enemy with a battle cry,
The General's wife, fierce in her command,
Led her people against the invading hands.

[continued]

[The General's Wife-continued]

Arrows flew and clashed on the ground,
The hiss of steel, a deafening sound,
Her heart pounded loud, a rhythm of war,
For her beloved estate, she'd fight to restore.

Through the chaos and strife, she stood tall,
Inspiring her troops to rise after each fall,
With every strike, she defended her reign,
A warrior noble, fueled by devoted love's pain.

Her eyes blazed with determination and might,
Protecting her home, their beacon of light,
The battle raged on, both fierce and long,
Yet she never wavered, her spirit so strong.

[continued]

[The General's Wife-continued]

She shielded her people, her loved ones dear,
Overcoming the hurt, overcoming the fear.
Victorious, she stood on the battlefield
scarred,
A testament to her strength, both fierce and
marred.

The General's wife, a warrior born,
A guardian of honor, never to be torn,
In the battle of her life, she had prevailed,
Her land protected; her valor unveiled.

For in her heart, she carried the flame,
A legacy of strength, a warrior's name,
Guarding her home, a heroine in strife,
So is the tale of the General's wife.

Forgotten

Out of haunted memory,
Beyond the sea of emerald green,
There is a place of sorrow,
In the Forest of Forgotten Things.

Singl socks are piled high,
As are pen caps, glasses, and loose change,
And even though there's clutter a plenty,
That's not the most upsetting thing.

Daring among the shadows,
Hiding in the trees,
Tiny little voices,
Echo out to me.

I see a little urchin child,
And I ask the boy his name,
He gives it and then runs off,
Unaware that mine's the same.

<u>***Survive***</u>

Why do you fear these scars,
Just because they don't look like yours.
Do you know how long it took me to make
them?
Shape them. Create them.

Why do you fear these scars,
Skin beautifully blistered and marred.
Survived the hurting and the beating,
Carries with it the memories defeating.

Why do you fear these scars,
Not the chains or whips or bars,
That stung the flesh,
But now I rest,
Under a blanket of these scars.

On this side of my skin,
It doesn't matter if I'm fat or thin.
It doesn't matter if I'm rich and tall,
On this side of flesh walls.

On this side of my eyes,
Every smile is a sunrise.
Every laugh is a deep breath,
On this side of my head.

On this side of my nose,
Smelly cheese is a summer's rose.
A warm embrace the perfect home,
On this side of my bones.

On this side of my skin,
I'm beautiful when I grin.
I'm perfect even with my sins,
On this side of my skin.

A Honeymoon of an Odd Nature

"Tick-tock," says the clock,
As Death impatiently taps his foot.
Death, he waits for no man,
But today he had to stop and take a look.

It was a rumbling, bumbling Tuesday,
And every house lit up the block.
A parade perhaps, or a wedding,
Regardless, they were a funny stock.

A man dressed in a white gown,
The woman in black slacks,
And trailing right behind them,
An angry mob right at their backs.

The gentleman, he giggled,
As the lady swaggered on.
She turned to taunt the henchmen,
That had come to burn the lawn.

[continued]

[A Honeymoon of an Odd Nature-continued]

The merry little couple,
Waltzed right on up to Death,
With bright smiles, eyes that twinkled,
And whiskey on their breath.

"We're here. We're here."
They rambled on, as if it was a jest.
Death shook his head befumbled,
Until he saw the red upon the dress.

He'd collected many, many a folk,
In his long eternal life,
Yet none had left him so perplexed,
As the male bride and his wife.

<u>*Fires*</u>

Lake of fire burns and boils,
Thrash and fight, trouble and toil.
Light the beacon, flood the dam,
Running savage across the land.

Foolish pride can't be contained,
Poisonous greed left untamed.
The thought that mercy is just a jest,
And wonders why there's such unrest.

Angry warnings, threats to homes,
Make it seem like we're all alone.
Hollow hearts, empty heads,
Hell is real when we're already dead.

One-step, two-step, left foot, right,
They planned it all out one drunken night.
Women in the kitchen cooking,
Men in the office or factory working.
Children like dolls, seen and not heard,
And it flew across the land just like a bird.
The system was built, the math had been done,
Follow the path, and your life will be won.
Conform, confine, and never cross the line,
Do all this, and you will be just fine.

[continued]

[American Ideal-continued]

But then came the outliers, the couple, the few,
Things didn't work out despite the plans that
they drew.
They must not have worked hard, they must
have done wrong,
The plan always works, just follow the script
like a song.
The system was built with such detail and care,
Follow it or fail, for the plan makes all of life
fair.

The mold was made, and not everyone fit,
And those that did lost all their wit.
For those that did not, it became open season,
For all manner of wickedness beyond all
manner of reason.
Fit in and maybe, probably, you'll be just fine,
Dare to question or not fall right in line,
They'll use it as evidence, and drown you in
blame,
You didn't conform and chose not to play the
game.
You followed your heart, and kept your name,
For that, they will laugh and call you insane.

<u>*The Winds of Time*</u>

Isn't it strange, the way the world keeps
spinning?
Isn't it strange, the way people keep on living?
Like time and space keep moving on,
No matter how bad things go wrong.

And isn't it weird, that people grow,
The way that people forget all that they know.
And isn't it strange, one day you're friends,
And the next day all that love suddenly just
ends.

Together forever and then you drift apart,
The love of your life is also the one to break
your heart.
Isn't it so funny? Isn't it so strange?
Isn't it crazy, how people can change.

<u>Limitations</u>

These prison walls I sit behind,
Boarders set in sand-drawn lines.
A caged bird's life is all I've known.
Shackles. Chains. I call them home.

Such sweet dreams dare to escape,
But wrinkles warn me I am too late.
And so I sit and fantasize,
About life beyond these sand-drawn lines.

Life's Great Balancing Act

Science and Spirit so often mistaken for two
separate things,
When, in truth, they are really one and the
same.
Just as Yin and Yang do not fight but flow,
The brain and the gut are comrades not foes.
The rise and fall, the give and take,
The highs and lows help soothe the aches.
Where would be the wandering heart,
Without the guiding brain keeping sharp.
And what, if anything, would the brain care,
Without a spark of love from the heart so fair.
To see the world in all its shades of gray,
And pausing to ponder what all it has to say.

<u>*Come With Me*</u>

Come runaway with me,
Where we can be wild and free,
Through fields of golden ecstasy,
With dreams as deep as the darkest seas.

Through meadows kissed by the sun,
Hand in hand, we'll explore unknown lands,
In each other's arms, we'll be undone,
Our hearts dancing to nature's commands.

Let's chase the horizon's fading glow,
Where the stars paint a celestial view,
With every step, our spirits will grow,
As we discover a love that's never cold.

So come runaway with me,
Where we can be wild and free,
Together, we'll rewrite our destiny,
In a world that knows no boundary.

Forget Me Not

Send out the fatal and the damned,
And watch them walk merrily in hand,
To which they'll go out door to door,
Delivering a hundred whips and then a
thousand more,
And when at last they've gone away,
We'll shake in doorways like a stray,
Shivering from fear and cold,
Until at last we dare grow bold,
The door left open, we dart inside,
And hear the whispers that start to rise,
We can't go back, the door is locked,
We're trapped inside, and voices mock,
They laugh that we're just skin and bone,
And from dead lips there comes a moan,

[continued]

[Forget Me Not-continued]

Our hollow moan, it echoes out,
Growing larger, into a shout,
This shouting, nay, it is a scream!
Of torment pure and deafening,
Skin splits apart and births our rage,
Hungry, savage, at last uncaged,
The voices speak but we don't hear,
Too long they fed upon our fear,
At last, the upper hand is ours,
We touch the sky and pick the stars,
Shooting stars weighed down with wishes,
For just one kind word and a few kisses,
What simple children we once were,
Until they came knocking on our door.

The Lake

I'll be at the lake.
When summer days have long gone.
When youthful tans turn wrinkled skin.
I'll be at the lake, with the drifting wind.

I'll be at the lake.
When crisp leaves fall down.
When frigid waters chill the toes.
I'll be at the lake, when no one else goes.

I'll be at the lake.
When I'm off in my own head.
When I need to disappear or fade away.
I'll be at the lake, where my soul likes to stay.

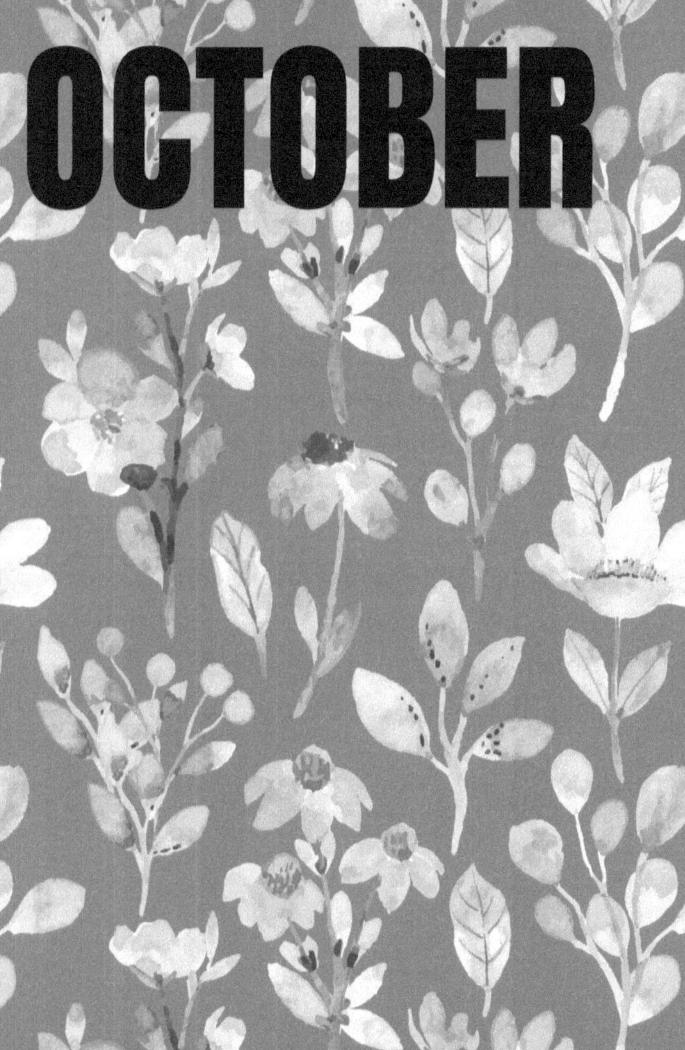
OCTOBER

The Demon's Plea

In shadows deep, where darkness dwells,
A demon's tale of caution tells.
With fiery heart and somber mind,
Warns love should never cross the line.

"Fair angel, keep thy distance far,
For love's embrace may leave a scar.
Though drawn to darkness, I reside,
A demon's essence lays deep inside."

"Within my realm, chaos prevails,
And to heaven's light, it surely pales.
With tainted soul and sinful ways,
I cannot lead you into this dark maze."

"The touch of love may burn your wings,
And to my realm, despair it would bring.
For demons thrive in wicked tides,
While angels soar where goodness abides."

[continued]

[The Demon's Plea-continued]

"I am the night, you are the dawn,
Two worlds apart, forever torn.
Our hearts may yearn, but never blend,
In this relentless battle, we must transcend."

"Though fascination sparks the flame,
Our destinies are not the same.
To keep you safe, I must refrain,
And let our paths diverge again."

"Fly high, dear angel, free and bright,
In skies untouched by my dark plight.
For love's allure may bear its cost,
A fallen angel, forever lost."

With pained regret, the demon speaks,
A cautionary tale that truth bespeaks.
In love's tangled web, they cannot escape,
A demon's warning of forbidden love's fate.

<u>Finality</u>

"It wasn't me!"
She said to the trees,
Out where the garden grows.

It was a chilly fall day,
At the beginning of May,
And heaven could only know.

There came a faint sound,
As she fell to the ground,
Little Darling, you'll reap what you sow.

Neither enemy nor friend,
Has say in the end,
Out where the garden grows.

<u>Darkness</u>

It is hunger, deep and raw,
It is a sorrow so consuming,
It is a shadow against the wall,
It is a twisted thought, confusing,

The space between the stars,
The depths of a craven man,
The colors of a war,
It cuts and bleeds and bans,

To be its haunted home,
To ache and burn with chills,
The pain to suffer all alone,
It's the darkness that will kill.

The Joker

Aces, Jokers, Kings, and Queens,
Playing games of liars and fiends,
Line them up and spread them out,
Defeated groans or triumphant shouts.

Stack the deck, shuffle, shuffle,
Distracted by the busy bustle,
Count them out, four thirteens,
Players aren't all what they seem.

The question is not the hand of cards,
Nor the strategy they guard,
The lesson here is just thus-
You'll never know just who to trust.

Boom goes the canon as the mighty fall,
Tat-tat-tat goes the bullets to end it all.
Hurry! Be quick! Don't hesitate.
There is a job to do, and we can not be late.
We chased the white rabbit down into hell,
Seduced and bewitched by his fairy tales.

And now we bleed into the mud and the rain.
Each death is a victory, a trophy of pain.
Howling dreams rip through the air,
They've numbed us down, so we don't even
care.
The smell of gunpowder forever lingers.
The feel of a dying man's clutching fingers.

We'll tell his family the most beautiful lies,
Thank our gods and then move on with our
lives.
But the boom of the canon still calls our
names,
And rabbit still steals the youth with tales of
fame.
The job is done, or so they say,
And now we are damned to face the day.

Buried Secrets Deep

The secrets I held in my heart,
Angry, twisted, and falling apart,
But a smile I wear to avoid the stares,
Don't get too close, best to beware.

The secrets I held in my heart,
They slowly rip me clear apart,
Can't deny this dry feeling,
Inside I'm broken and bleeding.

The secrets I try to hide,
Bury them down deep inside,
Can't let them out, can't let them win,
Hide the pain. Force a grin.

Witch's Prayer

Rabbit, frog, snake, and crow,
Oh, the things that they must know.

Rabbit, Lord of Winter, ruler of the Earth,
His time is that of the midnight hour.
God of blue, and death, and charity,
Master of death, with courage as his power.

Frog is Lord of Spring, ruler of the water,
His time is that of the morning light,
God of green, and birth, and affection,
Master of health, and kindness so bright.

Snake, Lord of Summer, ruler of the flame,
His time is that of the burning of the day.
God of red, and life, and victory,
Master of war, with sharp and cunning ways.

[continued]

[Witch's Prayer-continued]

Crow is Lord of Autumn, ruler of the wind,
His time is that of the gently dying sun.
God of yellow, and decay, and fear,
Master of messages, the most knowledgeable
one.

Rabbit, frog, snake, and crow,
Oh, the things that you must know,
Winter's skies that cough out snow,
Spring's sweet rains fall nice and slow,
Summer fires that burn and grow,
Autumn's breath that gently blows.

These gods are lost, but no one knows,
Where did they come from?
And worse, where did they go?

<u>*Mercy for the Devil*</u>

The darkness is so lonely,
The demons want to play,
The monsters are resigned,
They know what people say.

So easy to love a rose for her beauty,
But who respects her for her thorns?
It's a cruel little game we play,
But no one was ever warned.

Silence is preferred to stories,
And smiles over scars.
It's not so simple as a light,
It's the burning of the stars.

Who can find the mercy,
To show compassion to the devil?
Who can look upon wicked monsters,
And dare to say 'Hello'?

<u>*Thief*</u>

He robbed me of my youth,
Stole every minute of my day.
He took my peace, took my rest,
And worse, he's here to stay.

He stole the bloom from the rose.
He brought the darkness of the night.
He summoned every war I fought,
And now he's started to steal my sight.

Never was there a crueler man,
Who feels nothing of his crime.
I wish I had only known back then,
He was a thief called Time.

<u>*Laughing at Myself*</u>

What do you want from me?
I'm doing the best that I can.
It's hard to face reality,
When I'm sinking in the sand.

And how can I possibly,
Look myself in the eye?
When the stress is so suffocating,
Feels just like I could die.

It's harder than I thought it'd be,
Struggling just to be mediocre.
I once dreamed of being a king,
Yet here I am, the joker.

<u>Everlasting</u>

We don't have forever, but maybe just long
enough,
To forget, just for a moment, that we've both
run out of luck.
We have just meager minutes, before the
melting sun wilts away.
We never had forever, but for right now, my
Love, please stay.

We can immortalize a moment,
We can hold it in our hearts,
We can take this chance together,
Believe in new beginnings and fresh starts.

Yes, I know, darling dear, that the sun is going
down,
And soon will be the end, and we'll both
return to town,
And never dare to mention, or cautiously
speak a word,
This moment now is just for us, so let us forget
the world.

Of Loyalty I'll Die

I will follow you,
Yes, I will follow you.

I will follow you,
Yes, I will follow you.

Through the storm,
Into the cold.
We'll climb the mountains.
We'll trudge valleys low.
Through thick and thin,
I'll be there to the end.
An arrow to your bow.
Indeed, I will follow.

Just You

Flower vase against the wall,
And broken bottles too.
A time before, I can't recall,
I have always loved just you.

Burns and bruises are just pain,
Makeup can cover all the blue.
Tomorrow I'll do the right thing,
Because I've only ever loved just you.

Broken bones and broken homes,
It's the only world I ever knew.
My greatest fear is to be alone,
And so, I promise to love just you.

I hear the whispers, I see them stare,
And yes, what they say is true.
You've done more than I can bare,
But still I love just you.

About the Author

N. Cole Burke is actually a large, hermaphroditic, forest-dwelling toad that feeds primarily on coffee and Slim Jims. Once a month it emerges from its hovel and croaks ancient songs to the moon, such as Styx's Renegade or the Eagles' Hotel California.

This rare species of anti-social amphibian author prefers the solitude of its apartment over the clotted masses of crowds, though it has been known to venture out to the local bar from time to time. Especially when baited with half-off grilled cheese.

Isolated as it is, the creature is often left unsupervised with internet access and its own twisted musings. The 2020 quarantine was a particularly difficult time for the species and resulted in many first drafts and notes for future stories rather than any actual productive writing.

Wracked with guilt and a mild dose of self-loathing, the creature began working in earnest on completing its previously abandoned tales.

Between working a second and third job, and being distracted by the accumulation of random hobbies, completing said tales took much longer than had been originally anticipated by the toad. Luckily, as is the case with most breeds of writers, the N. Cole Burke is a nocturnal creature that often neglects sleep in exchange for 'Just one more page'.